The House in Harrison

Michael Andrew Marsden

Michael Andrew Marsden

PublishAmerica
Baltimore

First printing

ISBN: 1-59286-295-0
PUBLISHED BY PUBLISHAMERICA BOOK PUBLISHERS
www.publishamerica.com
Baltimore

Printed in the United States of America

ACKNOWLEDGMENTS

My thanks to Gail Rehfeldt for her skillful edit of my initial draft. I would like to thank my daughter Catherine Obert and my niece Barbara Kunze for reading the early drafts of this novel. My thanks to Sandy Whelchel of the National Writers Association for her critique of this novel. I am deeply grateful to the members of the Coeur d'Alene Chapter of the Idaho Writers League for their support, especially Marion Lillie and Mary Smith.

This novel is a work of fiction. All characters and the house itself are the product of the author's imagination. The town of Harrison is real. It has been for years one of my favorite places to visit. Located at a key position on the east shore of beautiful lake Coeur d'Alene, Harrison was the center of commerce for both the silver mining and the timber industry. Following the devastating fire of July 1917, the population quickly dropped from over ten-thousand to a few hundred. The Magnificat location, the rich history and the tragic fire combine to make it the perfect place for a ghost story. My sincere hope is that after reading this novel you will put Harrison, Idaho on your list of places to visit.

Chapter 1

"The house deserves a second chance."

Father David frowned. "What a ridiculous thing to say. A house is not a person, a spiritual being with a soul."

The old nurse shook her head. "I'm only telling you what she said. Mrs. Potter is out there, waiting in the hall."

The priest blessed himself. "That house was just a stage on which I played the role all young men must play, that of a fool."

"Father, she wants to talk to you. May I let her in?"

He paused and looked away out past the barren white walls to the window. "Why are hospital rooms so dull? The only color in sight is the light green of the maple tree's new foliage out in the parking lot. A sign of spring, a sign of hope."

The nurse stepped to the door. "Father David will see you but you must not stay long. He needs to rest for tomorrow."

Father David sat up as straight as the bed allowed. He cleared his throat. He watched as she slowly approached the side of his bed, an old woman struggling to walk with dignity but showing signs of the pain in each step. She stopped at the chair beside the bed but she did not sit down.

"I wish to buy the house in Harrison."

"Mrs. Potter, what do you know of the house in Harrison?"

The old woman sat in the chair before she answered. "It was the summer home of J. B. Marshall. When Harrison was almost destroyed by fire in 1917, the house was boarded up. I assume that no one has lived there since."

Father David nodded and closed his eyes. *The summer home. Yes, it was that. There were so many good times, when Mother was alive. It was after Mother died that everything changed. Even I was caught up in the change, fascinated by it, more correctly, seduced by it. But I was just a boy then. It ended in tragedy, as all inspirations of the devil must. But! But God did not destroy Harrison; a fire did that.*

He opened his eyes. "James Bradley Marshall IV was my father. After the fire, he assumed correctly that Harrison would not rebuild and he gave the house to me. I have not been back to Harrison."

Father David cleared his throat and looked more at the foot of his bed than at her. "When houses are left for a long period of time, especially in a small town, someone always starts a rumor about the former residents."

Mrs. Potter rose to her feet. "Now, if you are trying to renege on our agreement it won't work. My late husband worked for Potlatch Forest for forty-six years. I lived in a dozen different logging towns. Not one. Not a single one that didn't have a haunted house in town."

"Our agreement?" again a frown clouded his eyes. "I only remember saying that I would consider an offer for the house."

"Well, you have had plenty of time to consider it. You can't be very attached to a place you haven't been to in fifty years. I want to buy the house. I'll fix it up and live out the rest of my life there. What will you do with it if you don't sell it to me?"

"Do you know that there is a graveyard on the property?"

She nodded.

"It must be preserved."

She smiled. "I have no intention of disturbing the dead."

"Tomorrow I will have open heart surgery. My fate is in the hands of God and the team of surgeons. When I recover, I want to go down to Harrison and see the house again."

"You will be most welcome anytime that you wish to visit."

He rubbed his hand over the spot where he was told they would cut through the bones in his chest. "Give me the papers and call a nurse, we will need a witness."

Frank Potter paced the hall; like most young men he felt uncomfortable in a hospital. It was well past visiting hours. *Why had the nurse been summoned? What was she doing, that took so long?*

The door opened and Carol Potter stepped quickly out into the hall. She held up a packet of papers like a bouquet of roses. "I did it!"

"Did what, Grandma?"

"He sold me the house in Harrison. Oh, I've waited for this for a long time."

Frank watched as she carefully folded the papers and put them into her large black purse. Then he took her arm and they started slowly down the hall.

"Frank, when do you have to be back in Seattle?"

"I should leave on Sunday but I think I'll wait until Monday. I can afford to skip my art history class."

"Good. Sunday after mass I want you to drive me down to Harrison, Idaho."

Frank stopped at the elevator door and pressed the button with the down arrow on it. His grandmother held her purse in both hands like it was brand new. He was glad to see her excited about something again. She had acted so depressed the first year after Grandpa had died. It was a major blow to the family, having both Grandpa and Uncle George died in the automobile accident. The members of the family gathered closer to comfort each other. "Harrison, Idaho! Sure, it sounds like fun."

Chapter 2

The big Jeep station wagon rumbled across the narrow bridge over the Coeur d'Alene River. Frank Potter slowed for the curves as the car approached Harrison, Idaho.

"A mansion? Come on, Grandma! You can't even buy a good house at that price. What's wrong with it?"

"Well, an old house is often a good buy. They built them better in the old days. Don't listen to what your Aunt Connie says. This house was built by rich people. It will still be standing. I bought it from that priest. The one we went to see at Holy Family Hospital, Father David Marshall. He just moved back to Spokane. His father built the house in Harrison in 1912. He boarded the place up after a fire destroyed most of Harrison and David left for the priesthood. That was in 1917. No one has been in the house since. It was just forgotten."

"Hell! This is 1967 that's fifty years ago. An old mansion that no one has lived in for a half century. Is it haunted?"

"Slow down. You're coming into town," Carol cautioned.

Frank slowed the car as he turned the bend. His grandmother was not only of the other generation which always drove slowly, but her eyesight was failing and she could not judge distances very well. She still had spirit. Perhaps she bought this house to send a message to the rest of the family: no nursing home for me. "What's the population of Harrison?"

"Oh! It would be about 225."

"Big Time!"

"Now, Frank! This isn't Seattle. It is a nice place to spend the summer. You said you had nothing to do until fall. You wanted to get away from it all. A place where you could paint and not be disturbed."

"Oh! Did I say that?"

He only glanced in her direction as he spoke. He had wanted to leave the university campus; that was certain. Frank couldn't stand it anymore. Either he got another deferment and went to graduate school or he didn't get it and went to Vietnam. All the protests in the world wouldn't change anything. He just wanted to wait out the decision in some quiet place.

The road curved a little more and then rolled straight out before him. On his left up the hill from the road was a local bed and breakfast. To the right the lake front paralleled the road but a good fifty yards downhill. A block of commercial buildings replaced the scattered houses on both sides of the road indicating Harrison was indeed a town. Up ahead he could see a café. At least there was a place to eat.

"Slow down. I think this – yes. This is the place. Turn left at the next corner," Carol directed. "Up the hill. Slowly. It's a narrow road."

The road started straight up the hill and then turned a little to the left and continued as the hill steepened. Frank slowed to less than twenty.

"Slow down!"

She was right. The road snaked to the south, then back to the north, making a steady rise up and away from the lake.

"See that house?"

"Over there?" Frank looked right, then back to his left. The only house in view was off to the left and well below the road. Beyond the house he could see all the way across the lake to the steep hills of the western shore.

"That was the parson's house. It didn't burn in the fire."

"What fire?"

"Frank! I told you. In 1917 a fire started down by the lake in one of the sawmills. It spread all the way up the hill. Destroyed the town."

As the curve became more gentle and Frank could see further ahead on the road, he sped up. A short distance later he touched the brakes. "Hey! We're out of road."

Frank stopped the car where the pavement ended. Before him the gravel section of road continued to weave uphill growing narrower as it went.

"It's not too far. Go on," his grandmother instructed.

Frank drove another fifty yards, passing only one other house. It was a double wide trailer set on fill dirt off the shoulder. "Damn! Bet it was a chore getting that thing up here."

A big black lab ran out howling and barking. Two young faces appeared at the window. Frank waved and drove on slowly. The dog abandoned his position on the road and ran alongside the car for a short ways. Frank shook his head slowly when the dog finally turned and headed back to the trailer.

Sitting upright now, Carol looked sharply ahead as she spoke. "I'll have to check the records. I thought the property line crossed the road."

The road narrowed to a single lane as it turned again with only an occasional wide spot where another car could pass. The trees were more dense where the road crossed a draw. Frank slowed the car a little more as it splashed through a small creek. He guessed they were now on the north face of the bluff above the town. Trees guarded both sides of the road and grass occasionally invaded the middle section of the gravel.

"Frank! Turn right here. It's a sharp turn. See that house."

Frank looked to where his grandmother was pointing. There was a break between the tall pines. It was not graveled. It may have been a road once, but today it was just a grassy area under the pines. The ghost of a road led into a small meadow and beyond. There, only a short distance off the road, hidden in the trees, was an old house. Frank backed down the road a short distance and then started forward again. This time, as the car came forward, he pulled as far to his left as he felt safe before starting the sharp turn to the right. The power steering screamed but the Jeep station wagon lumbered through a hundred and twenty degree turn and headed through the tall grass. Frank tried to imagine where a road should be, if there ever was one, as he drove slowly toward the house ahead. "Should I put it in four-wheel drive?"

"No. That won't be necessary. Just keep going."

The closer he got the worse the house looked. Of the four windows he could see, the glass was broken in two of them. "Looks bad from here. Some mansion."

"Go on. That's the trick. Go on."

Frank drove on past the front of the house. There were no windows on this side, only two large doors. This wasn't a house. It was a barn or maybe a carriage house. Just beyond it hidden in the tall pines was another structure. "God Damn! It's a mansion."

"Don't curse, Frank. Yes, it's a mansion all right. Connie thought I was buying a pig-in-the-poke. Just wait until Judge Know-it-all sees this."

The mansion was a good fifty yards from the carriage house. The few tall pines that clustered near the barn guarded it from being seen from the road. The house sat on a small bench; the top of the bluffs could be seen just beyond. Dog-hair lodgepole crowded around the north and west sides of the house blocking a view of the house from those two directions. The lodgepole continued down the slope filling the draw they had crossed just after the paved road ended.

Frank parked directly in front of the stairs leading up to the front porch. The windows were all boarded shut. There was moss growing on the railing to the porch. He smiled. *A perfect place for a Halloween party.* "Grandma, have you ever been in there?"

"It's been boarded up for fifty years. I only got the key this week." She reached in her big black purse and pulled out a flashlight.

Frank helped his grandmother up the stairs to the house. She was a thin woman, tall for her weight but childlike beside his six-foot-four frame. As always, she was both hardy and stubborn. Still Frank offered her his arm for support, even though she would only admit to being sixty-something. Family needed each other. His family had seen hard years together and she was always the strength that pulled them through it. When his dad died in Korea, Uncle George tried to play the father role. But it was his grandmother who became his confidante. It was she who encouraged him to go on to college. Only she had anything good to say when he changed his major from science to art. After Grandpa and Uncle George died, it was Frank's turn to support her. It was therefore his duty to take her down to Harrison to see her newly-purchased house. They stopped at the door to the house and looked around.

It was near noon. Frank was grateful for that. The sun had climbed to its zenith and was doing its best to light the house despite the trees.

Even with the moss covering, both the steps and railing felt solid. The door was a massive piece of pine with no window glass. Frank had to open the lock. He thought the key would twist or break before it moved the tumbler, but with a loud double click it worked.

Once they were inside, the flashlight was needed. The shutters blocked all light. They moved slowly through the entry hall. Off to the right was a small waiting room with a built-in bench and a small fireplace. Then came a stairway with its heavy dark wooden banister. It went up a half-dozen steps to a small landing; then the stairway turned sharply back leading up and out of sight.

Frank slowly panned the light of the flashlight from the stairs across the ceiling in the hall. "A high ceiling! Must be more than nine feet! Hey, electric lights."

Frank quickly panned the light over the near wall until he spotted a light switch. He snapped a switch by the wall twice. The light above did not respond.

"Harrison had electricity back in 1917," Carol assured him. "I'm sure it has been turned off. You will have to check to see if the line from town is still there."

"And the wiring may not be code," Frank countered.

"They used copper wire back then, not that aluminum stuff."

"And they didn't use insulation."

"I don't feel like arguing with you. They left the furniture. I can't wait to see it."

Frank turned the light toward the adjacent room. It was a large room. The narrow beam of light from the flashlight was too weak to see well. Frank panned it slowly back and forth, with each sweep of light moving further into the room. There were huge grey canvas mounds on a dark carpet in the foreground, a fireplace, shuttered windows and the opening to the next room in the distance. "OK! Hold this."

Frank handed her the flashlight. He walked to the first grey mound and carefully uncovered it. To his surprise it was a loveseat.

"I don't believe it. Do you think this could be mahogany or cherry?"

"I'm sure it's mahogany," she replied.

He quickly uncovered the rest of the furniture. It was all good solid mahogany with fancy sticking, three loveseats, two chairs, a small table, and a piano. "Bingo! Get this stuff restored and you'll make a bundle."

"You still like to camp?" Carol asked.

"What do you have in mind?" Frank replied cautiously.

"I have a deal. I know a logger who might rebuild the road if I let him have the jackpine. Now your grandfather would tell you it was all pole size. He would also tell you any logger will try to take a few yellow-pine in the process. All of them, if no one is here to watch him. And Connie tells me that she knows a woman who restores furniture in Coeur d'Alene. This woman does good work, but I don't want her to have free access to the house. I need someone to be here. It may take all summer."

"You do have a problem with the people you deal with, don't you?"

"The best of society wasn't the clientele of George's courtroom these past twenty years. Your Aunt Connie won't do business with the worst, but she has some very useful contacts. You said you wanted a summer alone. All you wanted to do is paint. Well, I bet the carriage house will do just fine as an art studio. You can stay here after it gets cleaned up a little."

"A little! Hell! Just cleaning this place up could take all summer. Let's see what the rest of the house looks like?"

As Frank walked past the large stone fireplace, he paused. "Hear that?"

"It's just the wind in the chimney," Carol assured him.

"Or a ghost locked in the closet."

"Nonsense."

Frank waited beside the ornate pillars, where a center beam marked the separation from the adjoining dining room, until he felt her hand in his.

"They took the paintings too."

"What paintings?" Frank asked.

"Frank! And you are an artist. Every house has paintings on the wall. Even today. Let's move on."

This room was dominated by a pedestal table and chairs for ten. Against the far wall was a buffet that was taller than Frank. There was no china behind the glass doors however. Frank smiled as the beam of the flashlight sparkled off the crystal and brass chandelier that was suspended just above the table. "These people were rich."

"They took the china. I bet they took the silverware too. Let's move on, Frank."

Together they proceeded through the dining room to the kitchen. This was a simpler room with a long wooden counter against one wall, a stove and oven along the opposite wall, and a plain, wooden table in the center. Carol checked the drawers at the far end of the counter. "Looks like they took the silver."

Frank opened the drawer closer to him and took out a large carving knife. "They left the kitchen utensils."

As they walked slowly through the first floor, Frank was surprised at how modern it seemed. There was even a bathroom on the first floor. All the rooms were a little large by modern standards and the high ceilings made them look even larger. Opening a door in the kitchen that he thought might lead outside, Frank discovered a staircase leading down into the basement.

"Let's not bother with that now. We'll check upstairs," Carol told him. They passed on and went back to the stairs near the front door.

She took hold of his arm as they started up the stairs. The second floor had a bathroom at the top of the stairs. Then the hall led the way past four bedrooms to a second staircase. This one was more narrow and the stairs seemed steeper.

"Let's take a closer look at this floor first."

"You're the boss, Grandma."

Frank pushed the nearest door the rest of the way open.

"No, not that room. Let's check the next one," Carol suggested.

Frank walked down the hall and opened the door to the next room. "Wow! Look at that."

Unlike the main floor of the house, there was no canvas covering for the furniture. Frank panned the large poster bed with the narrow beam of the flashlight. The tattered grey remains of the canopy hung like moss on a tree. "Wish we could open that window and let some light in," Frank said.

He walked slowly around the large trunk at the foot of the bed. "What's this?"

"That's a lady's vanity table. Even then women wore makeup. A dresser, of course, and what was called a secretary's desk. And just to be sure your hemline was straight there is a cheval mirror," Carol told him.

Frank tilted the five-foot tall mirror and said, "Too short. After all these years I bet the bedding is shot."

He tapped the bedpost with the flashlight. "Solid hardwood bed frame. Could be cherry? Nice stuff. All you need is a new mattress. Hey! Look here!"

"What size do you think it is?" Carol asked.

Frank paced off the side and the foot of the bed. "Six and half by five feet – about the size of a queen size bed."

"We will need to measure it more exactly before I buy any new mattress."

Frank opened the closet doors and there was a pile of clothes on the floor and some still hanging on the pegs. He picked up a garment. It was a dress. "Women? Guess they left in a hurry."

"They left after the fire. It was enough to scare someone to death. After the fire the town never rebuilt to be much."

Frank dropped the dress on the floor and pushed on the closet door. It shut with a double click.

"Couldn't have all burned down," Frank said. "We passed some old buildings in town."

"Most of those are brick and were built after the fire. For a town of a few hundred, remarkable. At one time Harrison had more than twenty-five thousand people. It was the center of lake commerce."

"Lake commerce?"

"Frank, you need a lesson in history."

"Well, this woman left in a hurry. First thing to do is get the damn boards off the windows." He tapped the window pane with the flashlight. "Hell! The glass is all right."

One of the other three bedrooms on the second floor was similarly furnished except the bed had no canopy. The other two rooms had beds without footboards at all. Neither had a vanity table nor a desk; instead they had larger chairs and larger dressers. Frank put one hand behind him as he led the way up the stairs to the third floor. He moved slowly judging if he was walking too fast by the pressure of his grandmother's hand on his own.

At the top of the stairs was a large room. Frank moved to the center where he could stand erect. The slope of the roof was reflected in the ceiling leaving two sides without windows. The far wall had four windows but they were all covered from the outside. The room contained only a few chairs and one low credenza all lined up against the wall. At the near end of the room were two doors.

"Hey! First sign of damage." Frank noted the dark streak on the wall near the center of the wall. "Bet the roof leaks."

He heard it again, a high-pitched cry like a cat at night. "Now you hear that?" he asked.

"I bet behind that wall is the chimney," she replied. "Look! Do you know what that is?"

Carol walked quickly to the credenza and opened the door on the right side.

"A record player," she said and took a large black disk carefully from inside, holding it like it was crystal.

Frank studied the wall behind him. The chimney would be about in the center; he figured that was about right where the stain from the leak marked the wall.

"Wind in the chimney," he mumbled as he walked to the near end of the room and opened both of the doors. These led to a bedroom just a little larger than the ones on the second floor. In one room was a big poster bed without a canopy. It did have both a vanity table and secretary desk. What set it apart from the ladies' rooms on the floor below was the large rocking chair positioned to look out the window.

"The price of climbing all those stairs?" Frank said. "A bigger room. I guess that's fair."

"And perhaps a better view," Carol said pointing to the rocking chair.

The remaining room was furnished about the same as the two men's rooms on the floor below.

As they made their way slowly down to the first floor, Frank looked carefully for other signs of damage but found none. This was 1967. The place may have been empty since 1917, and the roof only leaked in one spot. He couldn't believe it.

In the darkness beneath the closet to the room on the third floor she stood in silence holding a worn and dirty blanket close about her. At the sound of Frank and his grandmother's conversation, tears filled her eyes. "A voice. Another person. Oh God, how I have hated this silence."

She called out but her husky voice was too frail to carry beyond the narrow passageway where she stood. She had followed the sound of footsteps and voices as they traveled up to the third floor of the house but she moved so slowly. Her tattered dress tore in fragments when it brushed against the splinters along the passageway. Her steps were slow and deliberate each one requiring the full force of her mind and spirit.

Now certain that they had left, she pushed on the trapdoor above and entered the closet. From there she entered her room. "Free! Free at last from that prison – that labyrinth of hell."

The room was almost as dark as the shaft she had left behind but that did not deter her. She had learned to see with her hands. She moved across the room and cautiously down the stairs toward the main level. The doorknob to the front door turned in her hands but the door would not budge. She tried all the back doors only to find the same result. Somehow she was still locked away in the house in Harrison.

"It doesn't matter anymore. I am in no hurry to leave now. They will return," she said in her harsh dry voice.

Without a sound she slowly made her way back down to the lowest depth of her prison. Pulling her rotten blanket about her for comfort, she returned to her half-conscious state. "They will be back. They must come back."

When they got back outside, Frank tested the porch rail. It felt solid enough so he stepped up on it.

"What are you doing?"

"Just looking," Frank replied. He stretched his six-foot-four frame and reached as high onto the roof of the porch as he could. He took several swipes to clear the debris of pine needles.

"Just what I thought - a tin roof. I still don't believe it lasted fifty-seven years."

"The house was built in 1912, which was two years after the 1910 fire. The value of a roof that wouldn't burn was fresh in the minds of people then."

"It didn't stop the fire in 1917."

"Frank, must you always argue?"

"Perhaps I should be a lawyer instead of an artist."

"One lawyer in the family is enough. Your Aunt Connie practiced law for ten years. That was before she married George, Judge G. E. Parker. Now she's a judge. I still can't believe a daughter of mine is a judge. It makes it hard to talk to her. Enough about lawyers; we should get some lunch."

Frank backed the station wagon around and started slowly toward the road. "When can that logger friend of yours take a look at this place?"

"In a few weeks. I didn't tell him where it was. You will have to take him up here. And watch. He's slick."

"You talk like you are sure I will stay the summer. I have other options."

"I can hire a man named Smith, Billy Smith. He's a handyman. Let him take a look at the roof and anything else that needs fixing. He's not an electrician. We'll have to hire one. Kootenai Electric will send out a man to look at the house. They won't fix anything in the house but they will inspect it."

"What about the plumbing?"

"I didn't think of that. Maybe Billy can help there too. No, I'd better ask Nick. He may not be too busy. This high up on the hill they wouldn't have a well."

"I can heat it with wood for a while but I bet it has oil heat. There were registers in the paneling on the second floor and transoms on the top floor."

"Frank. You are so observant. What's your honest opinion? Is it worth restoring?"

"Yes and no. As a building it's a great old house, but after you restore it, no one will ever want to live there. So you would be wasting your money."

"I want to live here. That's why I bought the house. We will fix it up this summer and then move in for a year. If it doesn't work, I can always sell it. It will be worth much more if it's fixed up."

"You would spend the winter in Harrison, Idaho?"

"Yes, I would. I love old houses, especially this one. An old house is like family. I won't live out my years in a nursing home."

The station wagon drove slowly past the trailer. Again the dog sounded the alarm. This time three young faces peered out the window as they passed. "Great neighbors," Frank said. "I don't know if I should help you do this."

"Frank, if it doesn't work, I promise I will sell it. Just give me a few years here. That's not too much to ask. I won't spend that much to fix it up. You see. I can use cheap labor, ex cons, and indebted relatives."

The more Frank thought of the project the bigger it seemed. By the time he got to the café in town it seemed insurmountable, but he put it out of his mind. Lunch was something he could handle.

The café was an old wooden building built on the steep hillside. The front with its big glass windows faced the main street in town. Inside, the white walls made the main room appear large. They selected a table near the long cream colored L-shaped bar. The menu was simple enough, burgers or sandwiches. The waitress was short but cute, with long dark hair, tight fitting jeans and dimples. Frank ordered a burger and fries.

"You know. My old car just made it to Coeur d'Alene. That's a steep hill, and I may have to haul stuff up to fix the house."

"For the summer you can use your grandpa's pickup truck."

"That station wagon with four-wheel drive would be better."

"The truck will do better for hauling the furniture to Coeur d'Alene."

"Well, I still need some money. Got to fix up my car before I go back to Seattle in September, if I go back."

"You have seen Grandpa's truck. It has just sat around since he died. I tried to sell it. Anymore the dealers won't give you a thing for a used truck unless you're trading it in. I don't need to do that, I have the station wagon. What do you think I should do with the truck?"

Frank smiled. *What will you do with this station wagon? You shouldn't be driving at all. Well, the truck is still better than my old car.* "You win again. This summer I'll use the truck."

"Then you'll spend the summer here?"

"Yes, I have until September. Then it's either graduate school or the army. Bet I can make it liveable up here by then."

"At the end of the summer you get the truck either way." She folded her napkin and then looked across the table and asked, "You know what your father would do. He went to Korea, but he didn't complain."

"Yeah, and he didn't come back," Frank replied. The sting of that remark showed in her eyes. Frank looked away. The teenage waitress crossed the room. *She looks like maybe seventeen, much too young. Still, she is cute. I bet she is the oldest single girl in town. Surely she's the best looking. I'd better make friends or it will be a long summer.*

Chapter 3

Frank watched from the porch as the big D-9 Bulldozer started to back down the road. From here he could now see the lake to the west and the river to the north. Cutting the lodgepole and thinning the ponderosa was a good move. But there should have been more trees left. He counted the ponderosa pines between the house and the road. Seven big old trees spaced in an uneven line marking the boundary of the property. Seven! He was sure he had marked ten to be left. His aunt had warned him too, that all Gypo-loggers are slick. He waited until the big Cat had backed to the end of the road and then he quickly jogged down toward the trees.

The D-9 Cat packed the roadbed pretty solidly. There were enough rocks in the fill dirt to give it stability. There was no drainage under the road. The water might pond to the east side before it spilled downhill to the north

"Hey, Clark!" Frank called to the man in the Cat. The big bulldozer crept to a halt, the engine still grumbling mechanically.

"Shouldn't there be a culvert down there? Water's going to pond all along here," Frank yelled.

"Not my job. Culverts should have gone in first."

He stood up as if to survey his work for the first time. The driveway from the road to the house was a mixture of fill dirt and rocks. It formed a long narrow raised platform. Water would drain down from southwest behind the driveway but not past it.

"It will drain. See over there. Where we took out those big yellow-pines. We pulled the stumps and leveled the ground, so the logging trucks could turn around. The water will drain from there into the ditch. You got no problem."

He didn't wait for Frank to agree. He started the machine slowly down the driveway, the blade collecting the few large rocks sticking above the tracks.

Frank shook his head. So that's how 'Slick' did it. He not only took three additional big ponderosa pines, he pulled the stumps and had the bulldozer level the area. Frank walked down to the spot where the trees had been pulled and examined the problem. No trace that a tree was ever there. Well, it might serve a purpose. The water wouldn't pond too deep before it spilled over to the ditch.

You could see the mansion now from the road. With the lodgepole pine all gone, the house looked like a castle on the hill. It had an unrestricted view of the lake below the town and the even greater view of the Coeur d'Alene River as it entered the lake. Perhaps this is how it looked when the house was first built.

His grandmother had called Harrison the Queen City on the Lake. Frank tried to imagine a city of ten to twenty-thousand people many of them headed for the mines in the silver valley. It had been a working city, she said, with sawmills, shingle mills and box factories all lined up along the shore. At the same time it was a major port for the big steamboats that hauled both freight and passengers down the lake.

Out in the distance Frank could see a tug slowly marching north with several braids of logs following behind. It looked like a half-dozen little mill ponds floating slowly down the lake. When Harrison had been the location for a half-dozen mills, the braces of logs would have been stopping here. History? Up until now that meant England, Rome, or Greece. Places he had read about and never seen. How many towns in Ireland were burned down, never to be rebuilt? How many in Vietnam would he burn? Frank took the letter from his pocket and started to read it again.

"It will say the same thing, deferment denied - major not critical field. Time to stop daydreaming." He folded the letter and put it back in his pocket. "The timber has been cut and the road rebuilt. Now I should move into the house."

Windows were the first tasks. Frank found that they were all nailed shut from the outside. With a crowbar and a claw hammer he managed to free the shutters for the porch windows. A fifty-foot extension ladder was needed to reach the second and third floor windows, another major expense for his grandmother.

Once nails were removed and a few latches replaced, the shutters could be fastened in the open position. Their dark red stain looked impressive against the moss gray stain on the walls. Inside the house was still a dirty mess. He camped on the porch that night.

Cleaning the first floor, even Frank's rush cleaning, took a full day, but the house was now habitable.

"Not good enough for Aunt Connie or Grandma, but for me it will work," he said to the empty walls. He moved inside just in time as the late afternoon showers turned to a steady downfall.

"Rain. I don't need," he yelled but the clouds continued to roll across the lake. "Stop damn it. Billy Smith will be here tomorrow evening to fix the roof."

Friday morning Frank set his camping stove on top of the electric stove in the kitchen and fixed breakfast. He was just finishing when he heard a truck chugging slowly down the driveway to the house.

The over weight driver looked like Santa Claus working a summer job. He even laughed as he spoke. "Hey! Nice pad for a young buck! Ha! Ha! Hey! You try the water yet? No, you look too grubby. Ha! Ha! Connie Parker, the judge herself, sent me. She said there ain't no leaks. That right?"

The jolly old elf was dressed in bib-overalls and a red sweatshirt. After he turned off the motor, his moving wreck of a truck chugged twice and shuddered one before it stopped and the driver climbed out.

"Name's Nick. You got to be Frank. Let's take a look. Don't want no leaks when we fire it up."

Frank led him through the house to the kitchen. Nick looked at the fixtures there and in the bathroom. There was even a small pool of liquid in the bathroom tank. Frank then took him upstairs to check the bathroom up there. There was no sign of any leaks.

"Acid test is when we get some water through them pipes. Ha! It may squirt up everywhere. Ain't this fun? Ha! Ha!"

Nick insisted that he check the basement as well. Frank led the way with a flashlight. There were no windows for the basement. It was not the small cellar-like area Frank expected but a fully finished level of the house.

The basement was one large room, like a meeting hall, with a huge bar at the far end and a smaller room by the stairway which included the space under the stairs. Several tables and chairs were stacked along the wall opposite the stair way. Despite the bar there were no water fixtures in the main hall. The room under the stairs held the oil furnace and the water main outlet.

"Now we go witchin'. Ha! Ha! Ain't this fun?"

Using a willow stick with a lead weight at one end Nick defined a path from the mansion toward the carriage house.

"Well that lousy son of a bitch! Look here. He drove that Cat right over them. Now that ain't right," Nick complained.

"What?" Frank asked.

"Don't you see? This here is a burial plot. One, two, three graves. Here's the markers. Damn! Can't even read'm."

Frank studied the area. The three pieces of wood must have been the substitutes for headstones. They formed a line except for the last one. The Cat tracks made a furrow through where the graves would lie, and had flipped the last marker out of formation. He picked up the rotten wood and placed it back in line. At one time it must have been more than six inches thick, now the bottom half crumbled in his hands. On the top side he could still make out the letters J-O-L-I-E.

"Hey! Looky here," Nick called from the carriage house.

Frank put the wooden marker back in line with the others and hurried over to Nick. On the back side of the carriage house was a door. It opened to reveal a small room. Inside was the connection to the main water line, a large holding tank, and a small booster engine.

"Bet your power line connected to this place too. They used to put all the utilities away from the main house. Ha! Ha! Ain't this something. This old piece of junk will never run. Ha! Ha! Wonder if it ever did? I can replace it. Got to. Got to find out how many leaks you got in your house. Ha! Ha! Ain't this fun?"

By keeping a close eye on Nick, Frank got trapped into helping. They quickly changed all the washers for every fixture in the house. In a few hours the water was back on line. No leaks were found in the house to Nick's disappointment.

Nick showed Frank where the fuse box was located, just inside the main door to the carriage house. He also suggested it be replaced.

"Son! I'd be afraid to live with this. Ha! Ha! It ain't no protection. Get it replaced with a new box, circuit breakers, separate lines for the kitchen, this here motor, and the furnace. Anything with an electric motor needs a separate circuit." With that last advice Nick mounted his diesel sled and departed.

Frank took time to lock up the house and the carriage house before he drove to town and called the only electrician with a Harrison address. The man argued that he'd lived in Harrison for ten years and that there was no such house. Frank repeated the directions but wondered if he would show up tomorrow.

"These steps are steep," Frank warned as he led Billy Smith up to the third floor of the house and through the ceiling access. The last passage almost proved to be impassable. The trapdoor that led to the roof itself was less than two-feet square. Billy slipped through but Frank found it a real challenge. He turned his body to the diagonal of the square and managed to get his head and one arm through. It was tight but he got his other shoulder through the opening and pulled himself up onto the roof.

It was a mansard structure. The very top near the chimney was almost flat. Beyond this in all directions the roof sloped away sharply.

"Here's the problem. Look at that! Damn! I bet the house was struck by lightning. You're lucky it didn't burn down."

Frank could see the dark pattern on the panel nearest the chimney. It looked like a crude drawing of the Columbia River's path, the mouth being the chimney itself.

"You're in luck. This being the top panel. Piece of cake. All I gotta do is put a new one over it. Caulk around the chimney. Done."

Frank studied the map for a moment.

"The leak wasn't that close to the chimney. It was about four feet out."

Bill looked skeptical. "So what you want?"

"Can we remove this and look under it?"

"That won't do nothin." Bill protested.

"I got a crowbar downstairs, if you can't lift it."

"Hell! Crowbar." Billy slipped the hammer from his belt. He knelt down and used the claw end of the hammer to loosen one side of the panel along what Frank saw as the west coast of Washington. Once it was removed, Frank's question was answered. There was a two-foot chamber around the chimney. The stain on the top wooden cross structure mapped the path the water had taken from near the chimney to the side of the chamber.

"Just what I thought," Billy said. "Didn't have fireproof insulation back then, so they left an air space so the heat from the chimney wouldn't cause no fire. Now if this thing don't fit back, it's your fault."

It did fit back. To Billy's annoyance Frank shadowed him as he made four trips to his truck and back before he finished fixing the roof.

"Next problem is power," Frank declared as he watched Billy Smith back his truck up and head down the road.

The electrician arrived looking around and shaking his head as if he still didn't believe the house was here. After a quick inspection he declared not only did the place need a new transfer box, but the whole house should be rewired. Frank balked at that suggestion. When the man added that he would have to pull all the old wire to make room in the chase for the new wires, Frank took a firm stand.

"A new fuse box, yes. No way you are going to pull that copper wire."

"Hey, it ain't code."

"How much will you pay me a foot for the wire?" Frank asked.

"Pay you! Bull! You pay me to wire the house."

"Sorry, no deal. I do appreciate you coming all the way up here to look at it for me."

"Buddy, you got no choice. You got to replace all that wiring. It ain't code."

"That's not what Kootenai Electric said."

"They been out here?"

"Yep." Frank lied.

"Well, if it's OK with them. I can replace the box here. Give you a good deal too. Put in a twelve box with a master."

Frank looked at the old fuse box. He counted the pairs of wires slowly. "One, two, three, four,."

"Hey! That's not it." The man pulled the main wire that went to the mansion. "See here, they got six other pairs of wire that ain't being used. Now they didn't have washers and dryers back when they built this place. You will want them on separate lines. There is eight, nine, ten, twelve. You need a twelve box."

By Sunday the roof was fixed and the water was turned on. Although there was a new control box for the electricity, Kootenai Electric hadn't come out to inspect it yet. Frank gave himself the day off.

He washed up but didn't shave. It had been almost a week since he had shaved last. He could wait another few days until he would have hot water. With a feeling of relief that he had the day off and a touch of hunger, he started out to hike down to town for breakfast. The big black lab at the first house ran out to greet him. He didn't bark until Frank was directly in front of the trailer house. In response four young faces appeared at the front window. The dog barked louder but as long as he was wagging his tail Frank just continued to walk.

"Hey, Napoleon! Come here."

Frank turned his head at the voice. The dog spun around and took off. It entered the trailer at a gallop. The man in the doorway said nothing to Frank but he watched.

"Morning!" Frank called out. He waved. The man watched. The oldest of the four little girls in the window waved back. Frank continued his walk into town.

There was no sign on the door of the café saying when it would open. Frank peered inside and could see a light on in the kitchen.

"Better be soon," he told the door and decided to go down the hill to the dock and look at the boats moored there.

A long wooden ramp divided the web of floating docks. To the right the wooden fingers of the public dock combined with a jetty on the shore to form a protected area for swimming. This morning the beach was deserted. To the left were the private docks as indicated by the presence of a bar-lounge-general store. The rest of the permanent residences were all just under 16 feet or just a little longer than that. It all seemed a feeble shadow of the once proud lake commerce his grandmother described. There were no steamers of over a hundred and fifty feet with room for almost a thousand people. Then there were not a thousand people in town. Probably hadn't been since 1917.

Frank walked out on the docks and personally sized up the potential of each of the floaters. Only one really impressed him. It was a little wooden runabout with a small cabin, white hull with mahogany trim. A comfortable boat for fishing or just cruising. The small brass plaque said, "Skiff Craft of Ohio 1956." Over ten years later and it was still the best looking boat in the harbor. Frank checked his watch. It was just after 8:00. "Hell! You got to be open now."

He started back up the hill to the café. The door was unlocked and he was their first customer that day. The little dark-haired waitress had on a yellow cotton blouse and white jeans.

"Gee! Everybody dresses up for Sunday," Frank said as she approached the table.

At first her eyes blinked in surprise; then she carefully put the glass of water on the table. "Good morning, Wolfman."

"Wolfman?" Frank smiled a the quick rebuke.

"That's what Jill calls you. We live in the house just down the road."

"Oh! In the trailer," Frank said.

"It's not a trailer. It's a double-wide home. And it's really nice inside, just like a house."

"Sorry! I was just surprised," Frank said giving his best bearded smile. "I see the little girls looking out the window every time I go by.

Each time it seems there is more than the time before. How many children do you have?"

She stepped back, grit her teeth, and held the coffee pot a little higher. "Do you want coffee?"

"In the cup," Frank answered quickly. "I'll rephrase the question. How many sisters do you have?"

"Six. I mean five."

"Really. That is remarkable. You should get an accurate count."

"I have five sisters, if you count me that makes six. I'm the oldest. Now do you want cream?"

"Yes, and sugar too."

"It's on the table."

"What's the special today?"

"No specials on Sunday."

"Make it bacon, eggs, toast and pancakes."

"Toast and pancakes?"

"I haven't eaten all week."

"I bet." A smile brought out the dimples in both cheeks. "How do you like your eggs?"

"Sunny-side up."

"Anything else?"

"What did you have in mind?" Frank said with a grin.

"Orange juice, or milk?"

"A small glass of milk."

Dimples - that was a good name for her Frank observed as she departed. The breakfast was good by any standards. After eating his camp cooking for almost a week, it was a feast. Dimples never let his coffee cup get less that half full. She even found a copy of the Sunday paper for him to read.

The front page devoted more space to the protests about Vietnam than to the war itself. Frank turned to the sports section. **Ali gets five years,** was the lead story.

"A $10,000 fine for evading the draft! Hell, to him that's pocket money," Frank mumbled.

He turned back to the front page and began to read. Besides

Vietnam, war was about to breakout in the Middle East; there was already a little war in Nigeria; no good news anywhere.

By the time he finished breakfast the small café was filled. Several parties were led through the café to the back room to be seated.

When Frank rose to pay his bill he went down the hall and checked out the rest of the place. The back was a bar but this morning it was breakfast only. There was also a deck overlooking the harbor equipped with tables and chairs. Opportunities were better that he first assumed.

The server's name on the check was Anna so Frank used it when he paid the bill. "Thank you, Anna. The service was as enjoyable as the food."

She didn't look up at him as she rang up the bill until she had to count out his change.

"Here you are, Wolfman; six seventy-five, seven, eight, nine and ten." Having finished counting his change, she looked up. "Going back to your haunted house?"

"Yes, but I'm taking the day off. No work today. My name is Frank, just in case Jill should ask."

"Jill is only five. And until you shave, you will be the Wolfman. I heard some old lady was moving in up there. You her husband?"

"No," Frank laughed. "My grandmother bought the place. She and my aunt are going to move in this fall. I'm only here for the summer."

"Well, don't let the ghost get you."

"I've been there a week. Haven't seen a ghost."

"Have you heard one?"

Chapter 4

A light breeze followed Frank back up the hill. The higher he went the more often the breeze was joined by sudden gusts. After he reached the house Frank thought the hike was enough exercise for a morning and he spread out on his sleeping bag on the couch for a quick nap.

Breakfast with Dimples would likely be the highlight of the weekend he mused. *She is just a kid. Hell, she is still in high school. I've dated much sexier girls in Seattle. Yeah, like what's-her-name – that girl with the long, stringy, blonde hair and the biggest bust on campus. Lena Allegra Bedfort, she was the hottest thing on campus. Of course I never really dated her. I did dance with her once. Anna - what a simple name. She is cute, I have to give her that. Quick - witted too. I like her eyes and that dimple in her cheek when she smiles. Someday she could really be a doll. What would my friends say if I asked a high school girl out for a date? No way. Her old lady would go ballistics; besides there is nothing to do in this town. Dimples? I wonder if she has a steady boyfriend.*

She had listened from the narrow passageways behind the wall at the first and second levels of the house and heard nothing. Slowly she made her way to the top floor. Jolie pulled herself up into the closet on the third floor. This was the hardest way to leave the secret passageways but she had first to be sure no one was in the house. "This is my room," she said to justify her efforts.

She opened the closet door just a crack. The light was so bright she took a step back. She stood in the shadow and let the fresh air wash over her. Then, shading her eyes with the blanket, she stepped into the room.

The bed, chair and other furniture were there just as she left them. She did not remember the layer of gray that covered everything. She pushed the curtains aside, unlocked and lifted the window. But it slid shut. Silently she turned and went down to the bathroom, took the dowel from that window sill and returned to the bedroom. Then she opened the window and placed the dowel to keep it from shutting. "I like fresh air. Oh! Look at that. That can't be Harrison? It is so different. How long have I been imprisoned here? Did my cousins escape? Do I dare try to leave again?"

She let the curtains fall back across the window. Still the light was bright and she lifted her arm to filter the view with the lace of her dress sleeve. The breeze caressed her. She fought the chill. Any feeling, even pain was so welcome after feeling nothing for what must have been years. For a moment she looked down at her hands and wondered, "Pretty hands but a tattered dress?"

She stepped to the tall cheval mirror. She tilted it down a little, then back up. "Where am I? I can see the dress. Why can't I see my face? No. No, it can't be."

A gust of wind slammed the door behind her. Jolie jumped at the sound and then laughed aloud. "Oh! What have I to fear? A ghost in the house?"

At the loud bang, Frank sat up quickly. The sound came from within the house. Somewhere upstairs. Frank quietly checked the back door; it was still locked. He remembered having to unlock the front door when he came back from breakfast. He looked around quickly. No windows on the first floor were open.

With the crowbar in one hand, he started slowly up the stairs. At the landing he stopped to listen. Before each door on the second floor he listened again before he entered. Nothing.

When he entered the last bedroom on the second floor, he found the closet door was opened. Frank checked inside, not certain if he had shut it the day before. He looked around but saw nothing he was sure had changed. The pile of clothing on the floor had not been disturbed. He quickly went back and checked the closets of the other three bedrooms. Two were completely empty, one like the last one had women's clothes still in the closet. None of the windows were open; none of the furniture looked like it had not been moved in years.

Last he checked the bathroom. That window was closed. Frank

remembered that Nick had propped it open with a wooden dowel while they were working in this room. He may have closed the window but where did he put the dowel?

He stood in the hall and listened for a while. The sound must have come from within the house. Somewhere up here. Perhaps the third floor? It sounded closer than that but so far the house was empty.

Halfway up the narrow stairway Frank stopped and listened. Nothing. Not a sound, yet he knew it was different. It was not as he had experienced earlier this week when he and Billy were working on the roof. Something felt different. The next two steps squeaked under his feet. Frank hurried up the stairs. Once you are heard, it is better to sound confident than hesitant.

The big room looked just as they had left it after fixing the roof. Frank checked to see that the trapdoor to the roof was in place before he tried the bedrooms. The first room was empty. It was dirty, but old dirty. No sign of anyone recently touching any of the furniture. The closet was bare too.

At the last bedroom Frank stopped. His hand was on the doorknob but he froze. Something was different. He could feel it the moment he started to open the door. The door gave a little resistance as he pushed harder and it flung open.

Frank stepped boldly into the room. The crowbar confidently held in front of him.

An empty room greeted him. The window was open. A wooden dowel braced the window all the way open. With the door open the breeze hurried through and down the stairs. Frank laughed then stopped at the double click sound behind him. He wheeled and with the crowbar raised, he took a step toward the closet door. The door to the hall slammed shut with a bang and Frank almost dropped the crowbar. “Who! What!”

For a moment he stared at the empty room and then he laughed. It was just the wind. It had blown the door shut behind him and the closet door before that. It was just the wind.

He walked to the window and looked down. This room afforded the fine view. The distance to the ground was a good twenty-five or thirty feet. Someone had left this window open. It hadn't been he, nor did he remember bringing Nick up to the third floor. But Billy had come this way when they went up onto the roof. Frank glanced up. He didn't know how long this window had been propped open but the overhang of the roof would have kept the rain from coming in last night.

Frank again looked down. Someone could come in this way. All they needed to do was bring the ladder over from beside the carriage house and bingo. Aunt Connie was right. No house is safe when it's empty.

Frank lowered the window and locked it. "A locked window is a fool's safety measure." The sound of his own voice help dispel his fears. Frank turned as if speaking to someone in the room even though he saw no one. "Glass is easily broken. The windows on the first floor provided an even better opportunity for a thief. The only difference is I would know it had happened by the broken glass. With an open window on the third floor, one can come, go and return a second time. I'll put an end to this."

Frank went back downstairs and straight to the carriage house. He unlocked the front doors and carried the ladder inside. The carriage house had a dirt floor, but it was fairly level. The place was virtually empty. It looked like it had never housed a horse or a carriage. A large wooden packing crate was storied along the middle of the back wall.

He nodded as he again surveyed the room. "Grandma was right. The place would do fine as an art studio if the doors could be left open. Without them open the light would be too dim. I could use the top of the packing crates as a table."

Frank put down the ladder and with some difficulty walked the crate across the room to the wall by the window. Behind the crate was a painting with a busted frame. Frank put it on top of the crate and returned to put the ladder across the back wall of the room.

This done, Frank went back to look at the painting. It was the portrait of a young girl. The wooden frame was broken. Not a broken corner which would occur if it fell from the wall but smashed. "What happened here? Did someone hit you with a hammer or bat?"

The canvas had stretched and ripped in the center. At one time there had been a plate on the bottom of the frame but now only empty nail holes remained. "This is curious. Why try to destroy something and then keep it?"

The crate was heavy and still nailed shut. Frank made a quick trip back to the house for the crowbar. The top of the crate quickly released the nails and he poked his flashlight inside. Paintings and books! No wonder the crate was so heavy.

He laid then out in the sunshine just inside the doors. Four paintings - two portraits and two landscapes. One landscape was of a big house in some old city, old stuff, definitely not western. The other was of a harbor, again not a western location and representing a time of sailing ships.

Frank studied the portraits closely. *The two portraits are both of beautiful women. Very young women, dressed in fine gowns! The brass names plates identified the golden-haired girl as Dorene.* He rubbed his short stub of a beard with his left hand. "Dorene? Now where have I heard that name before?" He looked over at the other painting. "Aimee? Yes, that name too seems familiar but who was it? Very good art work, I have to admit. But I can do as well."

Frank picked up one of the books and then another. *Novels, I am sure of that, but they were not in English. French maybe Latin but they are not English.* Frank turned a few more pages. *I am sure these are not Spanish but they are a Latin language. French is the best bet for the script in these books. My high school Spanish won't help here.*

He looked again at the landscape and the seascape. *They too could be French towns. This might be a good place for an art studio, but it's no place for a finished and framed masterpiece.* He carried them all including the broken painting back to the house.

It was a self-appointed task. A strange hunt but he found nails in the walls where he believed the paintings had once hung. The seascape fit neatly over the fireplace. The landscape on the opposite wall. The three portraits along the wall between the entry hall and the living room. He only hung two. The broken one he set in a chair.

"Now, are you the people who once lived here?"

The room was silent.

"Three women? That accounts for three of the rooms. How about the other three?"

Still, silence.

"Hey, six rooms, but three graves. What happened?"

Frank hurried back toward the carriage house. There in the graveyard alongside it he studied the wooden grave markers. He knelt down to deciphered the names, Aimee, Dorene, and Jolie. All were dated July 21, 1917.

"The day of the fire! They all died in the fire."

Frank blessed himself. He was already kneeling in the grass beside the graves. "A silent prayer. I feel foolish but it can do no harm and it may do some good."

The portraits haunted him all afternoon. Frank made several trips from the graveyard, then back to view the paintings or back upstairs to the bedrooms. He found a faded blue gown or pieces of one. It could be the dress in the picture of Dorene. Aimee's dress was black and all three rooms had black rags that once had been dresses.

No white gown was found. Still Frank assigned the bedroom on the third floor to the girl in the broken portrait, Jolie. He returned to that room. The window was still propped open. Silently he stood by the window looking back down at the graveyard. "Something is wrong. The fire didn't burn this far so how were you killed in the fire? If you panicked and ran down the hill and got killed in the flames, they could have you brought up here for burial. Why here? Doesn't the city have a graveyard? Strange."

The empty room did not reply but Frank felt for that he had been heard. Twice as he descended the stairs Frank looked back over his shoulder. Each time he saw no one there.

He took the painting from the chair and looked at it closely. "All the other two portraits need is a good cleaning and maybe a little touch-up work and they will look better than the day they were done. This painting cannot be repaired. If it had been cut with a knife, I could do something. The stretched and ripped canvas was final. Too bad, for in a way she is the most attractive of the three. She has that quiet beauty like Dimples, I mean Anna. Damn, I've got to get that kid out of my mind."

Frank held the portrait out in front of him at arms length. "I wonder what you did to make someone so mad at you. You're not the prettiest of the three and yet …"

He tilted the painting as if she was turning away. "Hey, don't go. I was just appraising your many charms. Your hair is not so dark as Aimee's, but your face has those same fine features. Your figure is not so bold as Dorene but you are definitely beguiling. I know what it is. It is your smile that sets you apart from the other two."

Frank sat the portrait back down in the chair. He shook his head. "Well, it is half a smile. The rip in the canvas has divided your face. Dimples! You have dimples just like - what's her name - Anna. Aha! That must be my weakness. Didn't know that until today. But your name must be Jolie. Well, Jolie, I am going to save you. No, I can't make this new. I can paint another portrait. Just wait and see. You will be as beautiful as you ever were. Just wait and see."

It was not on his schedule of things to do. Indeed this was to be his day off, but Frank began a systematic search of the house from top to bottom. He looked through every dresser drawer, every closet, every trunk or cabinet. He listed everything he found by the room in which it was found. Not until he was finished did he place his lists side by side on the kitchen table.

"Top floor. Lots of women's clothes in the bedroom with the open window, some personal items, hairbrushes, barrettes, there were even a few pieces of jewelry. In the other bedroom there were no personal items, only sheets, blankets and towels. In the larger room there were a record player, records and two chairs. Second floor, again women's clothes in the two of the bedroom closets, personal items, some jewelry but nothing of real value. Still even to Frank a difference in the sizes and colors of the garments but even more a difference in the jewelry left behind showed these rooms were inhabited by women with very different tastes. The other two bedrooms almost empty. Why no men's clothing? First floor, paintings, books; I put them there. Some kitchen utensils, no food, furniture. Furniture on all floors. In fact, those were the most valuable items left in the house."

He stopped and said much louder. "Whoever lived here must have planned to return. They buried the dead. They took all the belongings of the three unknowns and they took all the food. They didn't touch the women's stuff but they did lock the place up. They planned to return. If they didn't, they would have taken the furniture. Why leave the women's clothes? Why not take them? The women were dead."

A strange sound, almost like someone crying, made the hair rise on the back of Frank's neck. It came from the front of the house. It was not the sound of a child crying but it had that chilling effect. He dropped the paper he was holding. He listened and then slowly turned. He had left the crowbar in the carriage house. He had no weapon but he had to act. In long strides he gained speed as he passed through the house to the front door. It flew open and Frank leaped down the stairs. The big black dog wheeled and ran off. Skidding to a stop, Frank yelled, "Hey! Come here."

The dog stopped running and turned.

"Hey! Doggie! Here doggie?"

The black lab peered back.

"Here doggie! Here boy!"

The strange whining sound answered him.

The mixed conversation continued between Frank and the dog and they approached each other. Then the dog stopped. He didn't retreat but whined and waited for Frank. They circled each other keeping the gentleman's two swords distance. When Frank turned and walked slowly back toward the porch, the big, black lab followed. He sniffed Frank's heels, ran off once, and then returned. When Frank sat down on the steps, the big dog came close enough to let Frank touch him.

"Nice doggie. Good boy. What were you doing out here? I heard you. What were you up to? Just checking the place out. Different isn't it? Bet we cut down your favorite tree. That's a joke, dog. Don't you have a sense of humor?"

Frank followed the dog as he explored the changes in the

property. "It looks different, doesn't it? I bet it smells different too. Someday this will be a lawn. When the bulldozer rebuilt the road, it pushed over all those small tree stumps. You will like it someday."

Then when the dog finished exploring and turned down the road, Frank followed as far as the carriage house and retrieved the crowbar. "This is probably the best weapon I have. I'll take it back to the house with me."

He shut and locked the door to the carriage house and turned and looked back toward the main house. "House? That isn't a house it's a Mansion! That's it! Rich people live in mansions. They would naturally remove anything of value that could be easily carried away, like the silverware. They left the furniture because they intended to return. Women's clothing, French books, and those three paintings were of lesser value. Perhaps, they belonged to the people who closed the place up. They belonged to the dead, the three women buried here. But their portraits were in the carriage house. Lovers! That's it. Frank! You are a genius! You figured it out."

He stopped in his tracks. "The fire? Did they die in the fire? Why? They did die. There was a fire. Bury the dead. No, there are still a few pieces missing. Jolie's portrait wasn't broken by accident; was it rage or sorry?"

He studied the house before him. The door was open. He had done that. He had the crowbar. *Now if only I knew who opened that window on the third floor. It could not have been Nick. It could have been Billy, or even the electrician. No one else has been in there. No one that I've seen anyway. What if someone snuck in while I was in town? What if someone was still hiding in there. No, I just searched the place from top to bottom. The basement! I didn't search the basement. What if I found a dead body in the basement?* Frank shivered. "The basement will have to wait until the power is back on. Did I hear a ghost? The damn girl, what-her-name. Anna, that's it. Anna is going to spook me yet."

He walked back to the house saying to himself. "You can't search very well with a flashlight. I'll wait until the electricity is on before I check out the basement."

Chapter 5

Monday a man from Kootenai Electric did a quick inspection and told Frank the power would be on by Wednesday. After he left, Frank drove to town and called his grandmother with the good news. "We've got power."

"Good! When can you bring up some of the furniture?" Carol asked. "I found a place north of here that does a pretty good job of restoring antiques."

"You want the stuff from the living room first?"

"Yes, bring the two love seats, the couch and the tables if you can."

"What about the piano?"

"Leave it. Really, Frank, there is no way you could get the piano up here. Besides these people restore furniture."

She gave him directions to a farmhouse just north of Coeur d'Alene where she would meet him.

Figuring that loading the furniture would be too difficult a job for one person, Frank again contacted Billy Smith. Together they managed to get most all of the furniture from the living room onto Grandpa's truck.

"Think we'd better tie it down?" Frank said after they set the last table upside down on one of the chairs.

"Naa! Just take it easy and nothin' will fall out," Billy advised.

Frank locked up the mansion and looked up at the cloudy sky. "With luck I believe I will make it back before the rain forecast to come this afternoon."

Two miles out of town Frank pulled off on the shoulder of the road. The load had shifted, and the table was bouncing every time he hit a bump. Frank crisscrossed the load with a rope and tied it down tight.

It took over an hour for Frank to drive the overloaded pickup up the windy two-lane road to Coeur d'Alene. He had no trouble with his aunt's directions and easily found the small farm just north of the city. The main house was a rancher with a porch on the front and north side.

Two older men in dirty overalls hurried to the dirt driveway and directed Frank to the large red barn a short distance behind the house. If the barbed-wire fence defined the property Frank figured, he could see from one end of it to the other as he stood in the back of the pickup. He unloaded the old furniture with the help of two older men who lived at the farm.

Carol watched but did not comment on the unloading of the truck. She did take inventory of the items and their condition. Then she gave Frank directions to a furniture store in Coeur d'Alene on Sherman Avenue where he was to pick up three new sets of box springs and mattresses. "Now, listen carefully. I could only afford to buy three bed sets. They are all queen-size. From the measurement you took they should fit. I want the new mattresses put in the women's bedrooms. I'm sure you can tell which bedrooms were occupied by women and which were men's from the clothing left behind."

"Not just clothing. I found some jewelry too," Frank told her.

"Did you find a necklace?"

"No, nothing big. Just ear rings and stuff like that."

"Oh. I want to see anything that you find in the house. Now take the beds down today. The heavy stuff I will have delivered. Expect a refrigerator and a stove early next week. Any problems so far?"

"Only one; the place is haunted," Frank replied as he started walking back toward his truck.

"I thought you knew that. All old houses are haunted. Anything else?"

"There is a graveyard behind the carriage house. Did you know that?"

Carol stopped and looked up at him and then nodded. "Oh yes, I had forgotten to tell you about that."

"It has three graves all marked 1917."

She continued to follow him around to the cab of the truck. "The year of the fire; remember that it's important. Are the markers still there?"

"Yes, but they only have the date and the names, Amiee, Dorene, Jolie."

Carol smiled and asked, "No last names?"

"No, there weren't." Frank paused and opened the door on the driver's side of the truck.

Carol nodded. "For now we will leave the graves alone. Are they well-marked?"

"The grave markers are just pieces of wood." With that Frank jumped behind the wheel and put the key in the ignition.

"Frank, would you fence off the area? I don't want the area disturbed."

"Grandma, I know who's buried there. I saw them."

"Frank?"

"Let me explain. There is a graveyard with three graves. Three beautiful young girls. All with the date July 21, 1917. The girls are French too."

With a laugh and a smile she asked, "And how do you know that?"

"I found three portraits in the carriage house. The names on the paintings are the same as those on the graves. Come see for yourself." He said out the window.

"Frank, you're so perceptive. This adventure may turn out a little different than I planned. I wish I could come down to Harrison with you but I can't. Not next week either - Connie took the keys to my car. Judge know-it-all says I shouldn't be driving. But I have another plan. Frank, I will be there before the summer is over."

"I'll show you the graves."

"And the portraits, be sure and take care of those portraits. I can't wait to see them. Anything else?"

Frank scratched his chin. "What did Billy Smith do?"

"Why?"

"I don't trust him."

"George told me that Billy was a one man burglary team. Hit a dozen houses one winter. Sold the stuff to support a drug habit."

"No wonder I don't like him. How come he's not in jail."

"Plea bargain and they recovered most of the things that he took.

He's from a nice family and everyone wants him to succeed. Billy deserves a second chance. Just watch him. He'll be OK." Carol assured Frank.

When Frank was in town loading the new mattresses on the truck, it started to rain lightly. The store supplied a tarp which Frank secured over the stack of boxes. Frank promised to bring it back his next trip to town. He didn't tell them that he had no idea when that might be.

On the way out of town he stopped at a Safeway store and bought some groceries and beer and the latest copies of Newsweek and Playboy magazines. The rain grew from a sprinkle to a steady drizzle by the time he reached Harrison.

The moment he drove up the driveway he knew there was trouble. He could see the fresh tire tracks in the dirt road at the entrance to the driveway.

"Someone came by while I was gone," he mumbled.

The rain-softened top level of the road clearly kept the tracks of another truck right up to the carriage house. Frank was certain someone had come there that afternoon, after the rain started.

He stopped the truck just past the carriage house and scanned toward the house. No truck parked near the house. The door to the house was still shut but the upstairs window was open. He drove on, turning the truck around and backing it up to the front steps.

Frank hopped out of the pickup and hurried to the door. It was locked. He ran around to the kitchen and checked the back door. It also was locked. Frank circled the house checking the damp ground. No tire tracks or footprints. He checked carefully where a ladder would have had to be placed to reach the upstairs window. Except for some dog prints there was no sign of that a visitor had been here.

Frank looked carefully at the tracks his own truck had made. Whoever it was came well after the rain had started. More important they hadn't driven up to the house itself. Just the same Frank unlocked the door and did a quick walkthrough of the house. The dining room furniture was there. The kitchen looked untouched. The second floor looked no different than it did for his last search of the house. The third floor also looked unchanged. Unchanged! No. The window was wide open. Propped open with the wood dowel just as it had been on Sunday.

"Damn! I wish I had remembered to close that window. If I knew what was worth stealing, I'd know where to look," he commented aloud. "The furniture maybe? But why enter from the third floor?"

Frank returned down the stairs still looking for something that was gone. He put his groceries away in the kitchen. It took another hour to get the mattresses and box springs up the stairs. As instructed Frank put one set in each of the first two second floor bedrooms closest to the stairs. He disassembled the old beds and forced the old mattress into the new mattress boxes.

"This has got to be trash. No one would try to rebuild an old mattress," he told the stairs as he made his first trip down. He continued out the door and tossed the mattress into the truck. Frank took a short break before taking the new box springs and mattress up to the third floor. Last he brought down the old box springs and mattresses and then loaded all of them into the pickup truck. Frank drove the truck down to the carriage house.

When he fumbled with the key to the padlock on the carriage house doors, it turned sideways in his hands. "Damn it!"

Frank slipped the lock off. It had been cut. A few metal filings and a jagged edge were the tales a hacksaw left behind. The lock had been put back in place and neatly closed so as not to be noticed until the doors were opened.

Frank didn't remember anything in the carriage house worth the effort to carry it away. He looked around. There was the old shipping crate. Except for the furniture there was nothing here or in the house worth stealing.

"The paintings! If that's what you came for, I beat you to it," he said.

Frank raced back to the house to see if the paintings were still there. They were. He returned to the carriage house and unloaded the first box springs. He dragged it across the dirt floor to the back of the room. No need to let trash block his light from the windows. He had the second box springs in hand when he stopped. "The ladder. The damn ladder is missing."

With the old mattresses still in his truck Frank drove to town and called the sheriff. He told the woman who answered the phone that he had the receipt for the ladder and he suspected that Billy Smith had taken it.

That night the black lab made his evening visit. He timed it just about dinnertime and got a share of Frank's baloney sandwich. After dinner Frank read some of Newsweek. Moshe Dayan had led Israel to victory in just six days. Russian-built tanks were destroyed or abandoned across the desert landscape.

"Now that's the way to fight a war. Fight to win, or stay out of it," Frank told the black lab. He skipped past the articles on the civil rights gathering in Newark. New Jersey seemed farther away than Vietnam. Westmoreland was calling for more troops that Frank figured would seal his fate. He was doomed. There were some photographs of Jayne Mansfield. Frank read only far enough to learn that she had just died in an auto accident.

He tossed Newsweek aside and picked up the copy of Playboy. The black lab jumped at the flying magazine and headed off across the muddy yard between the mansion and the carriage house. David watched him go and at the same time watched the sheriff's car drive up the road. Billy was sitting in the front seat with the deputy.

"You got trouble, kid," Billy said as he got out.

"Where's the ladder?" Frank asked.

"God Damn! Asshole! I just borrowed it."

"Stole it," Frank countered.

"You calling me a thief?" Billy yelled. "Nobody does that."

"Hey, calm down. Are you Frank Potter?" the deputy asked in a friendly but assertive tone.

"Yeah. I'm the one who reported the ladder stolen."

"Now, Billy here says he just borrowed it. Going to return it tomorrow. Said he had been helping you fix the place up. He didn't ask because he couldn't find anyone around."

Frank shook his head slowly. *Whose side are you on? Hell, man you act like this is a simple misunderstanding. Well, it's not.* He answered in one word. "Bull!"

Frank pointed at Billy and raise his voice. "He knew I would be gone. How about this?"

Frank held up the lock that had been cut open.

Billy turned and looked off toward the carriage house. "He's lying. The place was open. It wasn't locked."

The deputy took the lock, and the bill of sale Frank had for the ladder and nodded his head slowly as Frank explained what had transpired that day.

The deputy again nodded when Frank finished. "I heard that Judge Parker had brought this house. Are you related?"

"George was my uncle."

"Then Judge Connie is your aunt?"

"Yeah."

The deputy nodded once more and then he turned to Billy. His tone of voice changed a little, and the warmth was gone. "Billy! You just can't stop, can you? Now, you're still on parole. You just don't learn do you?"

"I told you I borrowed it. I don't know anything about that lock. Maybe he cut it."

It stayed light until after nine, the benefit of northern Idaho summers. Frank worked off his frustration by cleaning the bedrooms on the third floor. He was mad at Billy. He was mad at his grandmother and he vent his anger as he worked. "Why did she bother with such people? Hell! That deputy isn't much better! He didn't arrest Billy. I bet they just go have a beer together in town and share some fatherly advice? Billy had better come back with the damn ladder tomorrow."

That night Frank spread his sleeping bag out on the mattress of the room he had just finished cleaning. "Got a new mattress but we don't have clean sheets. Or maybe we do? I'll have to check that linen closet on the second floor again. This stuff may be old but it could still be used."

It seemed stuffy to Frank after sleeping outside for a week. He opened the door and put the chair from the small desk in front of it so it would not blow shut. Before climbing into bed he paused at the open window. "I don't think it was Billy who opened this window. He would need that ladder to climb up here. It just doesn't make sense. I need an open window to let the night breeze in, but not this wide open."

He leaned forward and looked at the overhang of the roof. This window could be left almost all the way open. It was all right. If it rained again that night, things would still be dry. It might even make the whole house better ventilated.

He broke the wooden dowel over his knee. He lifted the window and inserted the bottom half near the side. "You get half, and the other half will go in the bathroom window. That way we get a flow of air through the upstairs at least. I wouldn't dare leave a window open on the first floor. Guess I fear a burglar more than a ghost." Frank tuned around and looked behind him. Seeing no one, he went to the bathroom and opened the window.

In the darkness of midnight a large grey owl glided silently past the window of the third floor bedroom. Jolie watched it with fascination. Her eyes now adjusted to the bright lights of the moonlit sky. She would leave. Go out into the night. Descend the hill and take a steamer to Coeur d'Alene.

She stepped to the bed and raised her dagger. *How easy it would be to kill this young whelp. He wouldn't even awake if I slit his throat. But who is he? He certainly is not a Marshall. He is too tall. What is this?* Jolie stooped to pick up the crowbar that lay on the floor beside the bed. It was too heavy and it slipped from her hands. Frank jumped up in bed at the sound. He looked directly at her, then away, his eyes searching the room. Jolie stepped back quickly toward the doorway. Frank swung his feet to the floor and rushed to the window. Jolie gazed appraisingly at the tall, young, muscular body. When he started to turn from the window, she stepped quickly into the hall and waited, dagger held high. He didn't come out into the hall. She heard the wooden bed frame squeak and assumed he had climbed back into bed. For a while she just stood there listening.

Once she heard again the even breathing pattern of sleep, Jolie moved silently into the room. For a while she stood at the foot of the bed waiting. He was young, strong and so much bigger than she, but she had a dagger and he was asleep.

Without any warning he sat up in bed and looked directly at her. "Go away. You're beautiful but too young."

Then he lay his head back on his pillow.

Jolie retreated quickly across the room and into the closet. There she turned and looked back at the figure in the bed. "Beautiful Monsieur. Thank you, but too young? I assure you I have pleased better men than you."

The closet door closed tight. The double click of the door handle followed. Frank woke with a jolt. He scanned the room by the light from the window but saw no one.

"Damn you, Dimples. Did I hear a ghost? I ought to go down by your house and make noises. Did I hear a ghost? Bull!"

He reached down and felt for the crowbar. It was still there next to the bed. Frank lay back down and was soon asleep.

The next day Billy brought the ladder back. He didn't say anything; he just stopped his truck and took out the ladder. By the time Frank had walked down to the carriage house, Billy had turned his truck around and was gone. Frank put the ladder back in the carriage house and locked it with a new padlock.

The electricity wasn't turned on until Friday. Then with power it was time for exploring the basement. Frank began to systematically replace all the bulbs upstairs in the house. He made a point to replace the bulbs before turning on the light switch. In only one room did he encounter a problem. In the last bedroom on the second floor the lights flickered and went out when he flipped the switch. He checked the bulbs and flipped the switch off and on again. The lights still flickered bright to dim. Frank changed the bulbs with no improvement. "Something wrong here. I'll fix it later."

When he finished with the rest of the house, Frank descended the stairs into the basement with a bag now only half-full of new bulbs. Because it was so dark in the basement, he flipped on the three light switches when he reached the bottom of the stairs. The room remained in darkness. The beam from the flashlight located the nearest wall lamp. Frank removed the old bulb and replaced it with one half its size. "Light! It worked."

He still left the flashlight on and proceeded around the room. Eight wall lights, and they all worked. The two chandeliers each held six lights. All the sockets worked but two.

"Now, that is a miracle," Frank proclaimed. He wondered if old light bulbs were valuable.

The basement was not as dirty as the upstairs. Perhaps the lack of air circulation was the reason. It felt damp and musty down here. He surveyed the large room. "The oil furnace should be replaced with something more fuel efficient, but how would you get a furnace down the narrow stairs from the kitchen? Somehow they had brought the oil furnace down here, but how?"

Frank walked slowly around the basement. Except for the small chamber under the stairs it was one huge hall. The stairs entered from one side and there was a stone fireplace along the other wall. The bar was at one end with some small doors behind it. At the other end was a single set of double doors, but there were also doors along the wall just past the stairs.

Frank paced the length of the room. Fourteen paces, that would be just less than forty-two feet. The width was just under ten paces. There were no windows in the place. The walls were all pine; they looked like they had once been lightly stained.

He walked back to the bar and looked down the room. "The double doors at the end of the room are the best bet for an exit to the outside; but I don't remember seeing an entrance when I was in the yard."

He walked behind the bar and began to check each door as he went clockwise around the room. Behind the bar the doors revealed a lattice structure which may have once held enough wine bottles to quench the thirst of all of Harrison. But it was now empty except for a dead spider or two. To the side near the stairs the doors gave entry to full-size closets, one of which held two tabletops. The adjacent closet held what was probably the legs to those tables plus a broken chair.

He walked around the small furnace room and the stairway. Finally he arrived at the far end of the room and the double doors. The crease at the level with the door handles had been splintered. Frank could just get his fingers between the doors. He pulled but the door held. Frank went back upstairs and got his crowbar. One hard jerk and the doors separated giving entry to a stairway.

"Damn! I didn't see any outside entry but there must be one."

He pulled the right door all the way open. The left dragged on the floor. Frank put his shoulder to it but it still refused to move. "Damn poor workmanship! Hey, there's the problem."

Frank bent down and wrenched a metal poker from under the door. "This belongs in the fireplace. That damn Billy! Hell! First the window on the top floor. Now this. He's clever, but I still don't remember any basement door outside."

Frank left the basement, hurried up to the kitchen and out through the back door. He had to circle the house to find the location he wanted.

Litter, more than fifty years of pine cones, needles and branches, had cumulated to cover the entrance. Frank scuffed his feet and kicked at the likely location until he found something solid under the forest duff.

Once he located it, he used the crowbar to clear the outline of the wooden doors. They should have been elevated above the level of the ground around them but the pine trees had combined to level the area with needles and hid them well. There was a door handle but no lock. With a little tug the handle pulled out to the wood below. Frank used the crowbar to wedge one door up a little so he could get a hand under it. The door creaked and groaned but opened before it broke loose from the hinges. Frank pushed it aside and opened the other door.

The dozen cement steps led down to the open panel doors and the basement where he had just been. No fear of cement steps decaying with time, so Frank reentered the basement. "This place never ceases to surprise me. Now I want to know where all these doors lead."

The remaining doors opened to smaller storage areas. What they held only the owners would have known. They left no clues behind.

Frank returned the poker to the fireplace. For a moment he just stared at it. *I wonder if it still works? Of course it will, but I should clean this chimney and the one upstairs before starting any fire. A fire isn't needed now that it's summer but it would be nice this winter even after the furnace is fixed. I can feel the cool air coming down the chimney. It will take quite a fire to reverse that flow. It does mean the flue is open. And those ashes mean that there has been a fire here.*

"Now, that ain't right?"

He pulled the charred leg of a chair from the ashes. "With trees all around you, why burn the furniture?"

With the poker in one hand and the chair leg in one hand Frank slowly stood up. "Maybe. Just maybe. This wasn't Billy's work. I never took Billy down here."

He walked slowly back to the outside doors. There were fresh splinters that he had just caused with the crow bar. These were up high above the lock. Then there were the older splinters around the lock itself. Frank judged that they had been made long ago and the wood had darkened again with time.

"Someone tried to break out of here. It must have happened years ago. They tried. They failed. They were cold, and they burned the furniture to keep warm. Where are they now?"

Carefully he closed the doors.

Frank looked in each closet again. Then he looked behind the bar and moved the furniture. Frank turned, surveyed the basement room once more then shrugged. "Well, no dead bodies."

As he ascended the stairs Frank paused and looked over his shoulder. He saw no one but he felt he was being watched. He switched off the lights when he reached the top of the stairs.

Chapter 6

Saturday, when Frank drove to town, he not only bought his groceries, he also bought several bags of grass seed. He didn't think to buy a seed spreader. That afternoon, Frank walked around the muddy acre of land between the house and the road tossing grass seed. Most of the stumps of the lodgepole trees had been covered by the rebuilding of the road.

A few weeks later when the rains stopped and the sunlight warmed the soil, hundreds of small purple flowers appeared almost overnight. Within a week they combined with the light green of spring grass to create a beautiful meadow.

Frank moved his easel outside for several evenings and tried to capture the setting on canvas. He was delighted when the scene was invaded each night by three deer. The following weekend he proudly mentioned his creation to Anna.

"So that's why the deer have stayed out of our garden this spring. You built them a new dining place." She observed.

"It's cool. They come up every evening. You should come see them."

"Oh! What a wild idea for a Saturday night," Anna replied.

"It's cool. Tell Jill about the deer. Maybe she is not afraid that she might meet a ghost when the sun sets."

Anna smiled. "Pa told us not to go up there. I don't know if that was because of the logging trucks or you. I'll tell him about the deer."

Late Sunday afternoon the big black lab, Napoleon, came loping up the road followed by Anna's father. He introduced himself as Ben Holmes. Frank addressed him respectfully when he spoke not only because he was older but because he was the silent type, the kind of man Frank knew without asking didn't smoke or drink. Frank also knew without asking the rifle on the rack in the back window of the pickup was loaded. He seemed interested in the mansion, so Frank gave him the grand tour.

Ben acted as if he were impressed with the appearance of the house. Perhaps, Frank thought, this man knows first hand what hard work had been required.

"Got power. Kept the wire?" Ben asked.

"You bet; it's copper," Frank replied.

Ben nodded in agreement. He stopped to look at the painting that Frank had done of the deer in the meadow. "You do that?"

"Yeah, I'm an artist," Frank replied.

Ben studied the painting for a while then nodded. "That's just the way deer act around here. One of them is always watching you. Nice scene to have right outside your door. Good reason to live here."

The following week the girls came to visit as often as Napoleon. They would come up in the late afternoons to watch Frank painting in the carriage house. They all came except Anna.

At first, Frank observed, their mother accompanied them. She, too, seemed fascinated with Frank's skill. One day he did a sketch of Jill, the youngest of the girls. Later that week he transferred the sketch to a canvas and began a portrait in oils. It took three days from sketch to completed portrait for Jill was not one to sit still for any length of time. It not only pleased her mother but the other girls were eager for him to paint a picture of them.

After that Frank could do no wrong. The children now came unescorted to watch him paint a picture of the mountains, the mansion, or perhaps the boats in the lake. He always included a few people in the scene and told whoever was watching him that day that she was in his picture.

Mornings Frank spent working on the mansion, from cleaning to painting. Late afternoon he would go out to the carriage house and work on his art. That is when Napoleon and the girls would come to visit. His little visitors never came to the mansion itself.

Anna worked the afternoon to evening shift. Sundays were different. That day she worked the morning shift. Frank would have his Sunday breakfast in town and see her then. Each weekend she was a little more friendly. If she were not too busy she even stopped to have a cup of coffee at his table and talk.

"And who are you painting today?" Anna asked.

"Jolie."

"Oh! Is she your girlfriend?" Anna glanced up as two men entered the café.

"No, she's dead."

"Oh! I'm sorry." Anna started to get up.

"Not my girlfriend. Jolie. Come on up tonight and I'll show you," he laughed.

"Can't do that," she said.

"Bring Napoleon. He'll protect you."

"That dog! He's afraid of his own shadow. Anyway I'm not afraid. I just have other things to do." With that Anna was off to wait on the new customers.

That night Anna came up to the mansion with Jill, Heather, her two youngest sisters and, of course, Napoleon. They gathered around the two easels that Frank had set up and marveled at the torn portrait of Jolie.

"What happened to her?" Heather asked.

"I don't know, but I am going to paint her a new portrait. See I have already started."

"Will you paint me?" Heather said.

"I already did a painting of both of you. Rose is next. She promised to pose for me next week."

"You never asked me," Anna said.

"I always save the best for last. What do you think of Jolie?"

Stepping closer Anna titled her head just as the image in the painting did. "She looks too snobbish. I don't like that dress. It's vulgar."

"What's vulgar?" Heather asked.

"I don't know. Ask your sister," Frank countered. "I think the dress is beautiful, and the girl too. This painting was done when she was living in the house back there."

Anna folded her arms across her chest, still studying the painting. "You're making that up? How would you know who lived there?"

"I know. She really did live here."

"How do you know? You just got here," Anna asked.

Frank stopped painting and turned to look at Anna. "The fireplace in the background and the loveseat. This was just how the living room was arranged when I got here. That means the painting was done between 1912 when the house was built and 1917. I think that she is lovely."

"You said she was dead. How do you know that?"

"Her grave is just around," Frank turned and pointed to the near side of the carriage house, "Over there. I put a little fence around it."

Heather hurried off around the side of the carriage house with Jill and Napoleon in pursuit.

"Do you always make up stories?"

Frank chose to ignore that last remark, but Anna stepped closer so she was between him and the painting.

"A good story has to be at least half-true," he said.

Her eyes had an impish smile enhanced by the dimples in her cheeks. "Only half-true?"

Heather and Jill came running back to the carriage house. "Anna! Anna! There is a graveyard. People are buried there. Come see. Come on."

Heather took Anna's hand and led her out of the carriage house and around back. When she returned, her younger sisters wanted to run home and tell their mother. Anna departed with them and Frank returned to his work.

"Well, Jolie. Let me apologize for my friend. Your dress is beautiful. It's not vulgar. It is gorgeous. You look absolutely ravishing."

Frank paused and took a step back to view his work. *The white dress centered one's attention from a distance. It contrasted so with the dark stone fireplace and the deep blue of the love seat.*

Frank took a step closer and the focus of his attention should have shifted to the face. He glanced over at the old painting and the single eye stared back. *The head is turned enough that the image should have two eyes. Too bad someone smashed it.*

Frank tried to imagine a profile of a woman with her head turned just this way. *Where goes the nose? How wide the lips? If the creature was wholly of my imagination, it would be easier.* He stepped forward trying to see strokes he was yet to make on the canvas.

Frank tried to paint the left eye in as best he could. *It should not be a duplicate of the right. No real person had identical eyes. As for that dimple in her cheek it may be on both sides but maybe not? Well, Frank, are you creative enough to complete this devilish smile? The old painting won't be of much help.*

"What's the matter? Are you stuck?"

Frank turned quickly to see Anna standing behind him. He smiled, for she had returned alone. "Not now, I'm not. You are going to be my model. Now don't say no. All you need do is stand right over here and turn your head like this."

Frank positioned Anna next to the painting. She did not react to his touch. Her eyes were always on his. It seemed like only minutes to Frank. He nodded for he had captured the profile he needed, the profile of a young girl in a romantic pose.

"Frank, is it done yet?" Anna asked, her face still holding that dimpled smile.

Frank glanced at his watch. It was later than he thought. "Come see?"

Anna relaxed and then walked over to look at the painting. "Is that what you think I look like?"

"Now, remember it's not you. It's Jolie. Without you I couldn't have done it, but this is Jolie."

"I stayed around for this?"

"Hey, don't be that way. I'd love to do your portrait sometime."

"No, you wouldn't." Anna put her hands up on her chest just above her bosom. "I don't wear dresses like that."

"Do you have a dress?" Frank countered.

She didn't answer she turned and ran off.

"Hey, come back. I didn't mean that."

Frank looked at his paints and the painting. *I can't leave all this and run after her.* Again he called out. "Anna, come back here."

It was no use. She didn't look back. Above her dark clouds gathered; another thunderstorm was moving across the lake to cut short the evening sunlight by which he could do his painting in the carriage house.

"Not tonight you don't," Frank took the easel and carried it to the mansion. He set it in the living room and put some newspapers around on the floor. By the time he closed up the carriage house and ran for the mansion, thunder was booming across the lake.

Frank quickly returned to his portrait determined to finish using the oils on the pallet. The portrait of Jolie still lacked something. He stood back, then closer; he shifted to one side then the other.

"Transition, that's it. Up close, you look beautiful, for I am looking at your face, your dark blue eyes. From a distance I see the dress because it contrasts with the background so. What we need to do is link them."

He chose a smaller brush and the white color first. "Some jewelry might work. What would you like? A simple chain or a necklace?"

A flash of lightning lit the room to beyond midday brilliance.

"Who are you?"

She vanished with the light. Frank stared at the spot where he had seen her, a glowing twin of the woman in the painting. But unlike the woman in the painting the twin held a dagger in her hand. Frank stepped back, blinked a few times and then shook his head. The lights in the room flickered and with the next crash of thunder the room plunged into darkness. For just a second in the transition from light to darkness he saw her again.

"Who are you?"

Bolts of lightning danced around the house accompanied by the crashing sound of thunder. Frank watched the shadowy figure advance with each flash of light that filled the room as if entering through the walls. Thunder fell like a hammer and he felt the house shake. She held the dagger in her right hand, arm extended and the blade pointed directly at him. She was just a few steps away when she turned and looked back at the portrait. He tried to run but his legs just shook. His neck stretched as his head tried to run away not waiting for the body to carry it to safety. Darkness reentered the room with the same speed that had brought the lightning. Frank stood there frozen in place. He waited for the dagger. *Will it be my neck? My stomach? Or here in my heart? Damn it, go ahead and do it.*

The lights flickered and came on again. He looked around the room afraid he would see her at any moment, but she was gone.

Frank listened but heard only the sound of the storm. It was departing as quickly as it had arrived. Frank wiped the sweat from his forehead with his left forearm. He looked for a place to put the pallet and his brush; then he looked back at the painting.

"Oh my God! What was that?" he blessed himself and got paint on his forehead and his left arm.

He poked himself with the point of the paintbrush. "It was just a storm. Paint! Now, that's real."

He stared at the portrait. It was so like the image in the room a minute ago. "Damn storm! Scared the hell out of me. No, I'm not afraid. I'm not afraid. Not afraid of you - not afraid of a storm - not afraid of the army - I'm not afraid of anything."

He looked over his shoulder. There was no one there. He looked back at the girl in the painting. She was smiling, daring him to come closer. Slowly Frank stepped forward and touched the canvas.

"I am going to finish this portrait tonight. What would you like a simple chain or a necklace? A necklace? Fine, just don't try to scare me like that again."

He had no image in his mind. His fingers did the painting. The necklace must be placed so it almost reaches her bosom, still some distance from the white dress. He added a little silver, then blue. Slowly a diamond necklace took shape. It worked beautifully linking the dress to the face. To complete the picture Frank added an earring to the left ear.

"Perhaps a little too much blue for diamonds, but I like it. You like it too? Good! It's yours."

Frank added just a few light touches of white to the eyes giving them a little sparkle.

"Jolie, you are beautiful." He looked around the room. "Don't ever try to scare me like that again. I am not afraid of you. I'm like my father. I'm not afraid of anything."

From the stairs behind Frank, Jolie put her hand to the lips to keep from laughing. Such a funny boy, not at all like the man who did the original painting. He was so serious and so handsome. *Yes, the blue diamond necklace is just what the painting was missing. Someday he will come and see this painting. I know he will. He will come back. And when he does I want him to know I still have that necklace. He too was a foolish boy, trying to be a man. Yes, Monsieur, you have that same problem. I saw you with those children, acting at times like a father or a brother not knowing who you really are. But with her you were different. This Anna, who wants you to love her. I can see it in her eyes. Foolish boy, why can't you see?*

It was almost the end of July when Frank drove to Coeur d'Alene and brought his grandmother down to see the house in Harrison. By then Frank had hired a second electrician and had new lines put in for the refrigerator and stove. When Frank drove up the new road, he slowed the truck and proudly pointed out the lush meadow that was now knee-high grass and flowers. Just then a big black dog romped out of the tall grass with a soccer ball in his mouth. "That's Napoleon," Frank said.

The dog was followed by the three youngest of the Holmes sisters. They laughed and giggled as they ran past the truck.

"Just the neighbor kids," Frank told his grandmother. "They come up here to play."

He drove on and parked close to the house. Carol stopped on the porch for a better look at the meadow of wild flowers.

"Pretty neat," Frank said proudly. "I did that. I planted the grass seed anyway."

"But the wild flowers, Frank, don't tell me you planted them too."

With great pride Frank took his grandmother on a tour of the house. Each room looked so much grander now that it was cleaned. From the detailed carvings on the small desks in the bedroom to the long bar in the basement each piece of dark mahogany glistened with deep luster. Carol smiled in approval until they reached the carriage house. This had become the depository for anything Frank had planned to thrown away.

"This place is getting full," Frank acknowledged to his grandmother.

The carriage house was indeed looking more like a storage area than an art gallery. When the new appliances arrived Frank had gotten the driver to help him move the old ones out of the way. The out of the way place was the carriage house. It now also held all of the old box springs and mattresses of three beds.

"I can sell that wood stove for a pretty price," Carol told him. She didn't think that either the old springs nor mattresses had any value but instructed Frank not to take them to the dump until she checked further. "Now let's see that graveyard?"

Frank led the way around the carriage house. Carol just stood silently looking at the graves for a few minutes before she spoke. "It's rotten wood; it's not clear but you are right. It once said Jolie."

"Oh, believe me, Jolie is buried here," Frank assured her. "See the dates are all July 21, 1917. This is a graveyard."

"I can see that, Frank. Why do you think there are no last names?"

"After the fire they may have wanted to bury people as soon as they could. Maybe it was all one family who lived here? They all would have the same last name." Frank shrugged for he wasn't satisfied with his own explanation.

"Perhaps. Now here's another problem," Carol said. "This house didn't burn. They must have died somewhere else. Why bury them here?"

"Got me. Still you've bought yourself a graveyard. You know they were very beautiful women. I restored the portraits as best I could."

"Oh yes, the portraits. I do want to see them again."

Frank led the way to the house and showed her the three portraits. "I found these in the carriage house. Note the names, Amiee and Dorene. So this one must be Jolie."

Carol studied the three portraits for a while in silence.

"Oh my, Frank, these are priceless. Three young beautiful and foolish girls. Would you believe that I once had hair like that? Of course you wouldn't. It's been grey for so long. Where did you find these paintings?"

"They were in the carriage house." Frank pointed to the bottom of Dorene's portrait. "Look - the artist didn't sign his name only his initials, D. M., and the brass name plates carry only the first names. The same as on the grave markers. They must have all been the same family."

Carol Potter smiled and shook her head. "Three young women all about the same age living in the same house. All very attractive, they do look like they are related but not sisters."

"Why not, Grandma?"

"They are too close to the same age for one thing. Just look at them Frank. Do they look like sisters to you?"

Frank nodded slowly. She was right. They didn't look enough alike to be sisters. He had studied those faces and the shapes of the heads before when trying to replace Jolie's portrait. They were quite different. Still he was sure that there is a family resemblance.

Carol turned her back on the paintings and said. "I had a talk with the priest who sold this property to me. He's recovering slowly from his operation. He wants to come down to see the house. I'll bet he will be pleased with what you have done as I am. The doors, the trim, it looks great. Especially the basement, I like wood, if it doesn't make the room look too dark. Cost is the problem. I can't afford new wall paper. At least nothing like what they had here once. Can you strip it and paint the walls?"

"The whole house?" Frank looked around the room. "That may take more that a month."

"Well, start with the main floor. Then the second floor. If you don't have time to finish the third floor, you don't have time. I plan to move in the second week of September."

Frank shrugged. "I've got to report the week before Labor Day."

"You seem to have enough paintings around for an art sale. Guess our arrangement worked out?"

"It has worked. Doesn't matter now, as I am not going to graduate school. The army won't care. By the time I get out, I'll have to start all over again. Do you really plan to move in here?"

"Yes. Connie is threatening to move in with me. She says I am too old to live here along. This summer she has a full slate of cases to hear, but in the fall it will slacken off a little. She will not be serving on the bench in a full-time position after September. Connie will have to share the Third District chair with some judge named Epson, until they decide if they want three or four judges. It sounds like it's a financial problem, but it's really a political one. This house is my project. I won't let Connie's schedule stop me."

Frank took his grandmother's arm and they started for the front door. "Grandma, listen to me. I know it sounds crazy but the house is haunted. Now wait. Let me tell you why I say that. First it was the window. The third floor window. Someone was opening it at night. Then it was the basement door. Someone tried to get out that way. But lately, I have been hearing footsteps at night. Then it happened. I saw her. That woman. I saw Jolie. She haunts this house."

Carol glanced up with a smile as she replied, "So Jolie is haunting this house? Why not Amiee? Or better yet Dorene?"

Frank shrugged his shoulders. "I don't know but she is here."

"Come on, Frank; it's all in your head."

"That's what I keep telling myself but I sleep with that crowbar beside my bed at night."

"Frank. Now I'm surprised at you. I would think if a young man like you would love to be living in a house haunted by a beautiful ghost. It's romantic. You do know about romance?"

"No time. Work. Paint. Wait for fall."

As they walked past the other paintings that Frank had done that summer, Carol stopped to look at Frank's latest sketches. "Now, Frank! Tell me, who is this young girl?"

"Oh! That's just Anna. I do sketches all the time. It's the basic skill of an artist. Just practice."

"Just Anna? Just practice?" Carol smiled.

"She's just a kid."

"Now, Frank, is it the ghost of Jolie that haunts this house or

Anna? Even I can tell that they look somewhat alike."

Frank shrugged his shoulders. "She's never been up here at night."

"Oh, Frank! You live in such an innocent time."

"Innocent! Haven't you heard about Vietnam?"

"There were other wars," Carol replied.

Frank didn't want to argue and he saw in her eyes that she didn't either. He drove her back up to Coeur d'Alene and returned that afternoon. She promised to return in a week or two and if she could get someone to drive her there.

That night wasn't a Sunday but Frank drove down to the café for dinner. He scanned around the room until he spotted Anna. *Tight jeans, bobbed hair and dimples. She is just a kid.*

Still, his eyes tracked her as she approached and he could not help the warm smile that invaded his face. "Hi, Anna! What's the special tonight?"

"You wouldn't like it," she replied looking off across the almost empty room as if she was bored.

"What is it steak, and lobster?"

"Meat loaf and mashed potatoes." She still didn't look down at him.

"Well, I was close. I'll have the chicken-fried steak."

"Anything else?"

"How about a smile from the prettiest waitress in town?"

Her eyes stole a glance at his just before she answered. "The only waitress in town."

"Oh no! There's Lucky. I mean Billy, in the bar."

Anna's mouth dropped wide open. "She's over thirty."

"How old are you?"

The dimpled smile took over despite her attempt to stop it. "What do you want to drink?"

"Milk. Tall glass. Look, Anna; I didn't mean to say anything wrong the other night. If I did, I'm sorry."

She folded her arms and replied. "I own a dress. I have several dresses, and I'm eighteen. Next month."

"And you have a beautiful smile."

Frank persisted and by the time he finished his dinner he was back on good terms with Anna. She asked him if he wanted her to wear a dress when he did her portrait. He agreed but suggested teasingly that her mother would have to chaperone.

Anna's eyes glared at him but her smile remained. "It's not that kind of dress. Besides, I'm not afraid of you."

"Not me. Remember, the house is haunted. It also is getting dark earlier. I moved my studio to the basement."

"Oh my!" Anna laughed. "Little me, in a haunted house with the wolfman. Now you're just trying to get out of it."

Frank felt his chin. "Wolfman again?"

"I'm sorry," Anna said. "If you don't want to do my portrait, I understand."

His grandmother's words flashed through his mind so fast, Frank almost dropped his coffee cup. "Now, Frank. Is it the ghost of Jolie that haunts this house or Anna?"

"What's wrong?" Anna asked. "Choke on your coffee?"

Frank put down his cup and rubbed his throat. He nodded his eyes fixed on hers. *For just a moment there she looked so much older. Now what do I do? I can't back out of this.*

He swallowed hard, coughed and then looked up confidently. "I do want to do your portrait. You're so much - more mature - than your sisters. I was just concerned about you. See you Sunday night if you have the nerve? I won't be offended if your mother comes with you. It's all right. I mean that."

Chapter 7

It was just after six, Sunday evening, when Anna came to the mansion. Frank had finished his dinner of hamburgers, string beans and rice. On the chance that Anna's mother would be with her, he was drinking iced tea instead of beer.

Frank was still in the kitchen when he heard her steps on the porch.

"Hey! I'll be right there," he yelled.

Napoleon greeted Frank's rush to the door with a loud bark. Anna was standing on the porch still dressed in jeans but carrying a dress over her arm. Frank guessed it was her prom dress, for it looked long even folded over as it was. He held the door open with one hand and gave Napoleon a token pat on the head. "So you did bring a chaperone. You get to stay out here, fella. Good boy."

Anna wandered in a few steps ahead of him and she took notice of the small fireplace just off the hall.

"Want a quick tour of the house before we begin?" Frank asked.

"It is big. I have never been in a house this big. What's this for?"

"It's the entry hall. You stop here and wait until the servants tell whoever you came to see that you have arrived. A place to sit, a warm fire; they may even bring you tea while you wait."

Her eyes were wider than he had noticed before. She looked up, holding her dress close to her side.

"No servants today. I gave them the night off. This is the living room. Take a good look at this room; it is about to be torn up. My grandmother wants me to take down the wallpaper. We can't afford anything like it, so I'm to paint the walls a cream color."

Anna walked slowly looking at the painting on the wall, then to the big fireplace on the opposite wall. She touched the piano as she passed by. "Where is the furniture?"

"My grandmother has it in Coeur d'Alene. It's being refinished. The piano was too heavy for me to load into the pickup. Let's see - there is where one of the love seats goes. The other sits right in front of the fireplace. And of course there will be three chairs. Come on.

Here is the dining room. I haven't had a meal in this room yet. I eat in the kitchen with the servants."

Anna managed a dimpled smile. In the kitchen she seemed more relaxed. Perhaps the presence of dirty dishes and other appliances made her feel more at home.

"Upstairs are six bedrooms and the bathroom. This way leads to the basement." Frank snapped on the light switch at the top of the stairs. "Now! This way to the studio."

The light blinded Jolie. She stepped backwards until she bumped into the bar. There was someone with Frank. Judging only from his tone of voice, Jolie guessed it was a woman. They would be coming down here. Why here? Jolie felt her way along the bar. Her eyes were slowly getting used to the light. She had to hurry but her legs moved slowly. *I must make it back to the closet.*

Anna hesitated at the doorway. She looked down, then back at Frank. There was only a single light at the bottom of the stairs. It wasn't enough to light the stairway all the way up.

"It's safe. Go on," Frank said.

She went down as far as the bottom step and stopped. Frank stepped past her. He flipped the switches on the wall and more light flooded the room.

"I know just what you are thinking. A room with no windows. A perfect place for mischief. Don't worry. It's my studio. I put in extra lights. See - even a light bar."

Anna looked around the corner of the stairway. She looked down the long room but she stayed right there on the bottom step.

"There is no one here. Nothing to be afraid of," Frank assured her.

"I'm not afraid of you. You don't scare me." She walked ahead past him into the room. "A bar! Why would anyone want a bar in his house?"

She stepped behind the bar and looked across it at Frank. Frank moved to the chair and a table near the bar where his art supplies were neatly lined up. Well, if neatly wasn't the proper word, functionally might be it.

"Now, Anna, I thought that you would stand over there or sit in the chair if you like. Let's see your dress."

Anna stepped out from behind the bar and held the dress out in front of her. The smooth blue satin skirt came almost to her ankles as it belled out from the waist. The bodice was lace-over-satin and crowned with a white satin portrait collar.

"Excellent. You couldn't have made a better choice." Frank beamed.

"Where can I change?" she asked.

Frank looked up toward the stairs and then quickly said. "I'll turn my back."

"Oh, sure! With that mirror over there behind the bar."

Frank turned and looked at Anna in the mirror. "OK! You change down here. I'll go upstairs."

"What's in there?" Anna said pointing to the door at the end of the room.

"That leads to the outside. But you're on the right track." Frank walked quickly to the side of the room near the stairs. He opened the closet door.

"I took the chairs out of here. Had to check if they were OK. Madam, your dressing room."

Anna entered cautiously. No question the closet was big enough. Frank put a chair in the closet for her to sit on and then closed the door.

"Hey, there is no light in here," The voice from inside the closet protested.

"Didn't you ever get dressed in the dark? Just yell when you want out," Frank countered.

"OK, smarty! Just don't open the door until I'm ready."

Frank reached out and touched the door handle; then he thought better of it and stepped back away. He began to rethink his arrangement. With such a long gown, it would better if she were standing than sitting. It would be different if he had a sofa or some larger chair. Her gown would completely hide the small wooden chair. The dress was light blue. He needed a dark background. He could always paint one in later but it was so much better to start out right.

"Well, I did it."

Frank turned around quickly. Anna was beautiful.

"Anna, freeze. Don't move."

She needed no makeup or jewelry. The fresh look of a summer tan on her young face and the physical charms accentuated by her dress combined in bewitching him. Frank felt his body trembled. *She is only eighteen. I must not touch her. Damn, but I hate the boy who took her to the prom. Aphrodite with dimples.*

Frank took a step back and forced himself to view her as he had viewed the models that posed for his class in college. The white satin collar came just off the shoulders forming a shallow V. It was just the right accent point to center her head. The dark hair haloed her face and flowed down behind her shoulders. For such a small girl Anna had strong shoulders. A definite collar bone gave her a really physical presence. The portrait collar of the dress formed a bow-shaped crown above the bodice of the dress. The appearance of the bust line was enhanced by Anna's exceptionally narrow waist.

"Well, Wolfman! Can I move now?"

Frank put his hand to the chin and shook his head. "I'm Frank not Wolfman. You wouldn't be safe down here with Wolfman."

He stepped to the right and looked her up and down again. "OK! That is a beautiful dress. The perfect dress for you."

Anna smirked. She walked over to the chair.

"Do you want me to sit?"

Frank took a deep breath. His mind was slowly gaining control over his physical urges. Yet his voice sounded far away to him as he spoke. It was as if another person was speaking. "Let me explain. Tonight the first step and the most important is to make a few sketches. Second step, start a portrait, but I want you to pick one from the sketches. Let's start with a standing pose. We'll do the chair next so you can rest."

"You didn't do the others this way. You just painted a picture of them," Anna protested.

"They are not you. You are special." Now the voice he heard was indeed his own. He smiled and added, "Funny, I never noticed before."

"Not funny," Anna was quick to reply.

A glow of confidence replaced his urge to act. *I'm twenty-two and she's just in high school. I must keep control.*

The first sketch was of Anna standing by the bar. The dark wood of the bar was a better backdrop for Frank's benefit than the lighter pine wood of the walls. For the second sketch he had her in a chair with the dark wooden bar behind her. For the third sketch he had her lean against the rock wall that was part of the fireplace. He took an angle so that he had Anna half facing the fire as she looked his way. For this last sketch, Frank switched his pencils and newsprint for charcoal and velour paper.

"Pretend that there is a fire in there tonight," he told her.

"Pretend? Why not light one? It's cold down here."

"Next time. For the sketches just be tough."

All three sketches were finished in just over an hour. Frank was amazed when he checked the time. Not only his techniques had improved this summer but also his speed. Most of all he was being professional about his work despite the physical attraction that still warmed his soul.

"Now, Anna, remember when you look at these. This is not a camera. It is not to see you as you are but to see you as someone else sees you."

Her eyes grew wider as she looked from one sketch to the next.

"Oh! It's me and it's not me. Can I keep this one? I want to show it to my dad."

"Stand over there by the fireplace again," Frank ordered.

When she had resumed the same position as before Frank moved to the easel with the canvas. He quickly sketched her profile and the basic shape of the fireplace. The controlled smile was gone from her face. In its place was a relaxed smile of wonder, dimples emerged and a slight pout took her lips. The sullen changes that only the truly photogenic are blessed with.

Frank worked for another hour. She didn't move. She didn't complain. The time was well spent. Although the painting would need much greater detail, the primary elements were there.

"Come, Anna. Take a look. This is just the start. When finished the face will have even more detail than this sketch. The large rough stones of the fireplace wall make a strong contrast to the daintiness of the figure."

Anna stepped alongside Frank and lifted her head as she viewed the painting.

"I'm not dainty."

"You are compared to the wall. It is an ultimate contrast. Add the fire and we have it."

"You're more interested in a piece of art than you are in me."

"Wrong. Step this way." Frank touched her shoulder lightly and guided her to her right until she was directly in front of him.

"Now turn around and look at the sketch. Let me tell you how an artist sees it. The dark wall of rocks makes the dress stand out. More than stand out; it comes forward out of the painting. It gives it a third dimension. It has depth. Immediately you see a beautiful woman. She is clothed in a dress, but it's a woman you see, not the dress. The dress represents her modesty, her virtue. Her form is physical. She's alive. Again in contrast to the wall which has neither life nor virtue. Next, your attention is drawn to the face. I need to do more work on that. You are more beautiful than this. The face shows the intelligence, the awareness of life. She is looking at the fire which can be a force for warmth or destruction. Unlike the fire or the wall, she is aware of what she is, a woman. The portrait, Anna, is you."

"Is that the way you see girls? That's weird. My father would never say anything like that."

Frank leaned forward and whispered in her ear, "When it's finished, if you don't like it, I'll burn it in the fireplace."

"Oh! No! Don't do that." She turned quickly around to face him. "I like it. Let's finish it."

"Not tonight."

"But we have to. I work all week. I'd take time off but I need the money. I could come up here in the morning after I finish my chores at home."

"If you wish, but tomorrow I'm going to start steaming off the wallpaper."

"What?" She stepped back away from him.

"I told you. I have to take off the wallpaper and paint the wall upstairs. That's my next job. Now if I knew what morning you were coming, I could do that stuff in the afternoon."

"Oh! I'll be here Tuesday morning." She stepped forward and put her right hand on his chest. "Can I keep the sketch?"

"Which one?"

"All three."

She was looking up at him. She was so close she raised her eyebrows as she did. He felt her right hand on his side.

"Please?"

"OK!"

She tilted her head up a little and closed her eyes. Frank kissed her lips. He only meant to kiss her once, but her lips parted and pulled his closer. The ember deep inside him burst into flames. His body shook and he lifted her off the floor pressing her body against his. He felt her fingernails dig deep into the back of his neck. His hands felt the shivers that raced up and down her back. Then she pulled her head back and pushed herself down. When her feet touched the floor, the dimpled smile flashed across her face. She turned and walked silently to the closet.

Show down, Frank. You thought for a moment you had her but she was in control all the time. Don't rush things. Think of something else - the painting. Think of it this way. You are not suppressing your desire out of fear, just postponing the event. In a few days you leave for the army. Don't do anything you will regret. This is not the night.

While Anna was in the closet changing back into jeans, Frank forced himself to study his oil paints and plan what colors he would need. Like his major professor advised, Frank started with just three colors, cyan, magenta, and yellow. He had been well schooled that everything was a mixture of these. The soft blue of the dress would be a challenge. It was, he admitted, a more difficult way to paint especially on a project like this where he would stop for a few days.

"Hi!"

Anna popped into the room from the closet.

"How did you do that? You did it before, didn't you?"

"Did what?"

"The closet door."

Frank walked over to the wall. He took hold of the door knob and pulled on it. The door did not open. He turned the knob clockwise. There was a pronounced click of the latch. Frank then pulled the door open.

"There is a door knob on the inside too," Anna said.

"Oh! But! Why?"

"So you can get out."

"But it's a closet. You're not supposed to be in there."

Frank scratched his ear and closed the closet door. *Tomorrow I am going to check the other closets in the house. This place is strange. Doorknobs are an expense. Why would anyone put one on the inside of a small closet like this? Can't worry about that now; I should walk Anna home.*

Jolie watched as the two walked across the grass as far as the carriage house; then she went down to the basement. She had learned to come out of the passageways only in the evening and night. The bright light of day blinded her. For a long time she studied the painting. *Anna is a beautiful girl, the beauty of innocents. Not for long, I can see that. He didn't try to take you tonight but that only means he has another plan. Poor fool, he will learn that seduction is a woman's game.*

It was good that Anna didn't come Monday morning. Frank found that he had to go all the way to Coeur d'Alene to rent the equipment to steam the wallpaper. Frank figured that Anna must have told her mother that he kissed her, for, when she did come to the mansion to pose for him on Tuesday morning, Napoleon, all five of her sisters and her mother came with her. The girls watched for only a half-hour before they began to get restless. Frank opened the door to the outside and the younger girls made several forays out into the yard and back. Anna's mother and her sister Elizabeth, who was perhaps two years younger than Anna, stayed to watch.

Frank worked on the portrait in thirty-minute sessions, taking a short break for himself and his model. After four sessions he called it quits for the day.

"I may add a few touches tomorrow, but for the most part it's done. Let's leave it here. Next session is Sunday night. It will be a short one."

"It looks done now," Anna's mother said.

Anna looked disappointed, but she said nothing. Elizabeth and Anna were whispering as they walked home just a few steps ahead of their mother.

That afternoon Frank started on the living room. First he pushed the piano into the dining room before starting on the wall near the fireplace.

The paper came off in small pieces at first. As he moved a little away from the fireplace and as the room began to feel more like a sauna, longer strips of paper began to roll off the wall. Frank worked until he reached the corner and then stopped. He took time to open the windows and collect the mess from the floor. A twenty minute break and a beer later he started again.

An exhausted Frank dumped the unused water and left the steamer on the porch. He went back to the kitchen and got another beer, beer number four. The day was done. He didn't even feel like eating. He was so tired. He went to the living room intent on closing the windows but decided the place was still too humid. He sat down on the floor by the wall and rested a minute.

Jolie watched from within the secret passageway. *He is such a strange young man. He doesn't pace himself. He either works very fast and hard or he rests.*

The steamed-air penetrated the walls. Another feeling, Jolie could not bear to leave. She felt the warmth of the wall and held her mouth open to drink in the air and taste the steam. *Hearing, seeing, smelling, feeling how I crave to fill myself. This past summer I have changed from the almost immobile spirit to one who prowls this old house in Harrison like a cat. When he first pulled down those shutters and let daylight again enter this house I was blinded. After spending years in the dark labyrinth, my eyes burned. Now I delight in watching the neighbor children from the third floor window. He has done this for me. This strange boy named Frank has given me energy. The longer he is in this house the stronger I become. But he prepares this house for someone else. What will happen to me if he were to leave?*

There was a loud bang followed by Napoleon's barking. Frank jumped up from sleep. He raised his left hand and checked his watch. It was six-thirty. His few minutes of rest had grown to an hour. He rose from the floor and walked to the front door. Napoleon had come alone tonight. For some reason he had a disagreement with the hose to the steamer.

"No! No! Napoleon no!" The dog dropped the hose to the steamer.

"Come on in. I was just about to eat. How do hot dogs sound to you?"

The big black lab trotted inside.

"Revolting? Well, they are not really dogs."

Frank continued to the kitchen. Napoleon stopped, sniffed the air and then began to bark again.

"What's the matter? Hey! Quiet!"

The dog approached the fireplace. His bark turned to a low growl.

"Hey! Quiet!"

Napoleon sniffed the wall and growled again.

"OK! Out with you."

Frank hustled to the front door with Napoleon on his heels. Frank stopped at the porch as the dog continued down the steps. "Go on. Go home."

Napoleon came back to the door after Frank had gone inside. He barked once and then wandered away.

Frank boiled the hot dogs in water, and heated baked beans in another pan. He added the dogs to the beans and carried the pan to the table to eat.

After dinner it was still light enough to check his work. In fact the setting sun came in under the porch roof, through the open windows and washed the wall by the fireplace in a light yellow glow.

"A big lemon with a freckle or two," Frank said aloud.

A freckle? Frank set the pan down on the kitchen table and walked into the living room. *There are two freckles, both at the same height.* He moved closer. Frank leaned down and half stooped as he studied the holes in the wall. *There are two holes just inches apart and only a few feet to the left of the fireplace. The wallpaper must have covered them. But what was their purpose?*

Frank nodded his head. *Now I remember. There is a space around the chimney. Perhaps there was one around the fireplace too.*

He went out to the trash pile in the yard. He examined every whole piece of wallpaper. He found the one. When he brought it inside, it checked with the height. A dark spot in the patter of flowers with a hole. These holes were made after the wallpaper was on the wall.

Over hot dogs and beans Frank sought an explanation. Any explanation. *It doesn't make any more sense than doorknobs on the inside of a closet.* Frank got his flashlight and began a systematic search from the basement to the top floor.

There were fifteen closets in the house. Four of them had doorknobs on the inside as well as the outside - one in the basement that Anna had discovered, two on the second floor, each in bedroom closets, and one in the bedroom he was sleeping in on the third floor. Frank returned to the top floor.

"Now, this is the second time for you," Frank said to the room. "First the window, now the closet."

Frank stepped inside the closet. He turned on the flashlight. The door handle was there just below his hand.

"Now why would I shut the closet door? There is no light in here. It isn't a dressing room. There is a dressing screen in the room."

He flashed the light beam around the closet as best he could. There were no light fixtures. Anyone who shut the door was then in the dark. Frank touched the door handle. There was a single loud clicking sound as he turned the knob. The door didn't open. He tried again turning the knob, but the other direction again there was the loud click. Still, the door did not open. He pushed the handle down harder. There was a second definite click and the door opened just a crack. "Now, I got you."

Frank closed the door again. *If down will open the door, what will pulling up on the handle do?*

He pulled up on the handle until he heard the double click. The door remained closed. Frank slowly scanned the door with the beam of the flashlight. He stepped back a step as he did. His heel hit an uneven board in the floor.

Frank knelt and lifted the board as it protruded just an inch above its neighbor. The board and the next seven lifted up.

"Hey! A trapdoor! Shit! Where does this go?"

The passageway proved too narrow for him to find out. A quick check of the other closets with double door handles and three more entrances were verified. Frank laughed. "What have I found here? If these entrances are connected, one can go from the third floor to the basement. Is this the Harrison Catacombs? Are there a bunch of people buried down there? Wouldn't that be a surprise?"

Frank closed the closet door and stood back. "All these secret entrances must have been built when the house was constructed. They were kept small so no one would notice. I bet that they are connected. Hell, if you were small enough you could go from the top floor to the basement without being seen. The haunted house in Harrison! Haunted ain't enough. There's a secret here. Just when I am going to leave, this place gets interesting."

From just beyond the edge of light that penetrated the passageway

Jolie watched. *Leave Monsieur Frank? You cannot leave.* "You must stay with me."

"What?" Frank turned and looked behind him. "Someone here?"

He looked back as he slowly closed the entrance to the passageway. Jolie stepped forward into the light. He looked directly at her and then carefully he closed the trapdoor.

Jolie waited in silence. She waited until she heard the doors to the closet close. Then she lifted the trapdoor above and with catlike swiftness ascended into the closet. Peeking through the narrow slit between the closet doors she watched him as he got undressed for bed. *You cannot see me, but just a moment ago you heard my voice. If only I had known that sooner, I might persuade you to stay.*

Chapter 8

Frank enjoyed breakfast Sunday. Anna was her usual mixture of charm and tease. She wore the same yellow blouse and white jeans she had worn many times before that summer. Somehow today she looked older and more attractive. Five times she asked and five times Frank assured her that he had finished the portrait.

That evening about six, Anna's entire family gathered at the mansion and Frank presented to them Anna's portrait. He suggested that they have it framed. Anna's younger sisters all begged to have another portrait done of them.

"Sorry. I leave for Seattle next week. Still got a lot of painting to do." Frank laughed. "Painting walls, that is."

"You go to school there?" Anna's mother asked.

"I did. I even got accepted in graduate school but LBJ has other plans for me. I've been drafted."

"That's too bad," she said, but her husband Ben smiled as if he had just heard the best news of his life.

"Then are you coming back here?" Anna asked.

"No, I have to go."

"I mean after you get out of the army." Anna asked again, "Are you coming back to Harrison?"

Frank just shrugged his shoulders and looked away. *I haven't thought about coming back from Vietnam. Maybe I will come back. No, that wouldn't be fair to Dad.*

After thanking Frank a hundred times, Anna and her family headed down the hill. Napoleon was in the lead.

Frank sat on the porch steps and waited and waited. It seemed that time had slowed to a stop. Finally, Napoleon's barking announced Anna's return.

"Hi! I had a lecture from my mother. She likes you but!"

"But what?"

"But stay out of his bed. Ha! I told her. He thinks I'm just a little girl. Too young. Bet you don't know I'm going to college next year. This year I'm a senior. Honor roll too. Do you have a girlfriend?"

"I did. I don't now. Let's go inside."

"What?"

"There is something I want to show you. The Harrison Catacombs."

"Catacombs? This isn't a con? Hey! My mother said!"

Anna bounded up the stairs. Keeping three or four steps ahead of him.

"First the basement then upstairs," Frank said.

"What's this about?"

In the basement Frank had to coax Anna into the closet with him. Anna insisted she hold the flashlight. After he clicked the door handle shut, he pulled up on it. The back panel of the closet opened just a little. Anna cautiously pushed it further open. It was a narrow passageway that she could easily slip through but not Frank. Anna took the flashlight and stepped into the passageway. "Hey, this is neat. Does it go all the way around the room?"

"I don't know. Does it go up?" Frank asked.

"I can't see how. Maybe there are stairs around the corner."

"Wait! Anna, come back here. Come back!"

Anna slipped through the opening and into the closet. "You don't have to shout. I was right there."

"Anna! I can't go in there. What if you got stuck?" Frank warned her.

She clicked off the flashlight. Frank opened the door to the closet.

"Now let's go upstairs," he said.

Anna skipped along ahead of him up the stairs and into the living room.

"What now?"

"Upstairs," Frank told her. He now led the way. She followed a couple of steps behind

"Why are we going upstairs?"

"The bedrooms are upstairs. Now forget what your mother said. I found a closet up here with a trapdoor in it too. There are secret entrances all over this house. I was going to show you all of them."

Anna giggled and continued on. They paused to look at the

bedrooms on the second floor, but did not go into them. Frank told her that they, too, had entrances into the catacombs. Anna laughed as she followed him up the narrow stairs to the third floor.

"This room, I call Jolie's room," Frank told her. "I don't know why. Any of the rooms could have been hers. She is the ghost who haunts this house."

Anna stopped two steps from the foot of the bed. "You sure like to make up stories. Where is the secret passageway?"

"In the closet."

She smiled and walked over to the closet. "Oh yes! Just like the downstairs. Coming in with me?"

Anna turned on the flashlight, stepped to the back of the closet and felt the wall with her hand. Frank shut the doors, turning the handle down. Then he knelt down and lifted the door handle. There was a double click as the pins in the doors fell into place in the floor.

"This wall didn't move at all. No, secret passageway here," she said skeptically as she beamed the flashlight in his eyes.

"It's down here in the floor," Frank replied. At a point on the floor just behind where the two doors met, Frank lifted the edge of the panel. Anna stepped aside as the panel rose until it rested against the back of the closet. Anna leaned forward while shining the light down into the hole in the floor.

"Why, it's no wider than a laundry chute," she said.

Frank thought it was quite a bit bigger than a laundry chute and big enough for her to climb down. There was a ladder too. It was built onto the side of the shaft. The shaft was not deep. It probably only went as far down as the next floor in the house.

"I think this passageway leads all the way to the basement. I don't know why it was built. Crazy, ain't it?" Frank said quietly.

"Is this what you brought me up here to see?" Anna asked.

"Yeah. I think it's something special."

"You're weird, Frank."

Frank stood up and put his hand on the doorknob.

"The closet door won't open until you close the trapdoor," he told her.

Anna beamed the flashlight up in his eyes again. “You think this goes all the way to the basement?”

“Yes; now get that light out of my eyes. Hey, what are you doing?”

Anna knelt down. She slipped to a sitting position and slid her legs down into the shaft. “I going to look around.”

Quickly she descended until only her head remained above the floor level. Then she took the flashlight and tucked it into the top of her pants. Frank watched as Anna descended another five or six feet and then stopped. He leaned over and reached for her but she was gone. Only a little light reflected back up into the closet.

“Don’t go very far. Where are you now?” Frank asked.

He knelt in the dark and peered into the shaft.

“You wait up there until I see if there is a ladder leading down to the basement,” Anna instructed.

“I think you should come back.”

“This is neat. You should have told me about this before. I thought you wanted to make out. Why should my mother worry?”

The closet grew completely dark and Anna proceeded further away from the opening.

“There’s a passageway leading off that way.”

“Which way is that way?” Frank asked.

“I’m pointing that way.”

“I can’t see which way you’re pointing.”

“Oh! Hell! I am going this way. No ladder yet,” Anna replied.

Now even when he poked his head as far as he could into the shaft, Frank could see only darkness. He wished he had a second flashlight. He waited minutes, long minutes.

“I’m going to get a candle. I can’t see anything in here,” Frank yelled down into the darkness. There was no quick objection so Frank closed the panel. He managed to open the closet doors on his second try.

Frank knew he had only one flashlight but he did have candles. There was a candle-lamp on the table by the bed but no matches. The only place Frank could remember seeing matches was in the kitchen.

He raced down the stairs.

The matches were not in the cupboard where he expected to find them. He began to empty the cupboard in a frantic search. Still, no matches. Frank stopped looking. He tried to picture just where he had seen the matches.

A banging sound from the wall behind him stopped his search. "Oh God! She's trapped."

He dashed for the stairs; then he heard the sound again. It came from the front of the house and it was joined by a voice.

"Hello! Frank! You have some visitors. Come unlock the door. Frank!"

Frank hurried to the door and then stopped. He heard Grandmother explain, "We changed all the locks on the house, and that grandson of mine got the type that always locks. A safety lock he calls it. Damn nuisance is what they are."

He looked across at the stairs, then back at the front door. She was peeking in the window to the front room. Now he had to open the door. Frank fumbled with the lock and slowly pulled the door open just a little. Carol Potter pushed the door the rest of the way open and walked quickly inside.

"Now why would you have the door locked? You up to something?" She asked with a grin.

Frank shook his head quickly.

"Frank, this is Father David. He used to own this house. Father, this is my grandson, Frank."

"Good afternoon, Frank," Father David said and offered his hand.

"I didn't expect any visitors. It's getting late," Frank stammered.

"Father David wanted to see the house again and those portraits too. We can't stay long." Carol led the way across the living room. "I told you about the graveyard; well, Frank thinks these are portraits of the three women. Where are those paintings?"

"I removed them to paint the wall," Frank explained meekly.

At Carol's instruction, Frank quickly put the portraits of the three women back on the wall.

Father David took care to study each. "After all these years you must have had to at least clean these paintings. I am surprised at the shape they are in."

Frank kept glancing at the stairway.

The old priest walked back and forth looking at one painting then the other. He took his time as if he were all alone. He kept coming back to the first portrait on the left.

"Well, Frank?" Father David asked.

"What?" Frank replied.

"I said you must have had to clean the paintings at least. Were they in bad shape?"

"Those two I cleaned and retouched. They hadn't faded so much and just dried out. That portrait was damaged so badly I made a new one."

"This one?"

"Yes. That's Jolie," Frank said. The priest reached up and touched the side of the frame. He took off his glasses, put them back on and looked up again.

"For a moment I thought it was the original. You really captured the artist's style." The old priest nodded his head as he turned to Frank.

"I did it as a copy. Actually it's better than the original."

"In the eye of the artist," the priest said. He raised his finger and pointed at the portrait. "The necklace, you added that?"

"Yes, I did."

"Where is the necklace now?"

"There never was one. I just made it up," Frank answered.

"You made this necklace up? Imagined it?"

Frank could see the disbelief in the priest's eyes and in his grandmother's eyes also. "I made that necklace up. I found some clothes in the house and some jewelry. Nothing of real value. This necklace I just dreamed up. Looks good on her, doesn't it? She's a real beauty. They all are. Too bad they had to die in the fire. At least I think they died in the fire."

"They died in the fire. My father and I didn't arrive until several days later. They were already buried. No one ever mentioned that necklace." He paused, then turned and asked again. "You must have found it?"

"No, I told you. I made up the necklace. But they did die in the fire. The graves are right out there by the carriage house," Frank insisted.

"Then how did you know what it looked like?" the priest persisted.

Frank turned toward his grandmother but she was looking at the wall behind them. "These women, all three of them are buried in the little graveyard behind the carriage house."

Carol shook her head and turned back to Frank and asked, "When are you going to leave?"

Frank swore he heard something fall or land with a metallic sound. He stared at the wall behind where his grandmother stood. *Where is Anna?*

"Frank!" Carol said aloud.

"What!"

"I asked, when are you going to leave?"

"I don't know. Sometime this week." Frank looked back toward the stairway. He felt the perspiration rolling down his face and looked down at the floor. "Son of a bitch!"

Frank bent over and picked up a book of matches from the floor. "Now, how in the hell did they get out here?"

Father David frowned, his eyebrows wrinkling like little accordions. "Let's go see the graves."

Anna could stand up straight in the passageway. She reached up and discovered that the ceiling was just a short distance above her head. It was not so wide that she could walk down it. Instead, she turned a little sideways and shuffled along. Anna had gone only a dozen steps when she came to an even more narrow spot. There was a thick wooden pillar pushing halfway into the passage. She peered around the pillar and could see only darkness. Anna thought she could slide past. She put the flashlight in her right hand. She turned, facing the pillar as she squeezed past it. She could hear Frank saying something but she couldn't answer just now. The flashlight lit the passageway behind her, not in front of her. Anna shuffled forward anyway. As she cleared the pillar she took a longer step.

"Ahhh!" she screamed as her left foot plunged into space. Anna reached out with her left hand only to feel the flat side of a wall. Her hand scraped the wood but found nothing to grasp. She continued to fall until first her left elbow and then her back hit something solid. In quick response, she spread out both arms trying to grab anything in the dark. The flashlight hit the pillar before dropping straight down. Her right elbow struck something solid. Anna held on, one leg below her, the other stuck up in the air. At least she wasn't falling any more. Her right hand gripped the edge of the wooden ledge that had stopped her fall.

The metallic sound below told her that the flashlight had struck something far away. Anna realized she was wedged by her arms at the top of another shaft. The long pause before the flashlight hit the bottom told her that it was a deep shaft. She could see nothing in front of her.

"Frank! Frank! Help! Damn you, Frank! Oh! Help me!" Her voice was a whisper at first then louder and louder. She was exerting so much effort to keep from falling, she could not scream. Leaning back and supporting herself with her arms, Anna pulled her right leg toward her body. Then she let it dropped into the shaft. At least her back hurt less in this position.

Anna glanced down. She could see a soft light far below. She guessed the flashlight hadn't broken in the fall. It was still on. She spread her legs feeling for a toe hole on either side of the shaft. There was none. Her arms were locked so tight it was hard to breathe. She stretched her left leg forward until she touched the pillar. The surface in front of her was not flat but rounded. Anna reached out with her right leg. Her right foot found something of a toe hold. Anna lifted herself up a little. Her arms moved as she raised her body, and the pain across her shoulders lessened. Anna found a second toe hold for her left foot. Carefully leaning forward, she took more weight off her arms.

Now she could see the light below much better. The flashlight was lying on the ground still a long distance away. That must be the bottom of the shaft, Anna reasoned, and if the flashlight was still on it hadn't broken. When she looked up, it was so dark in the passageway around her, she closed her eyes to avoid it. If this shaft was like the first one she had encountered, there would be a ladder attached to the pillar in front of her. That was probably what her feet were now resting on, but what if it wasn't?

"Frank! Can you hear me?" Anna called out.

Her voice was not strong. It was too dark to yell. He couldn't come to get her anyway. The big bear could never get around that pillar. Anna looked up and then closed her eyes again. Putting her weight on her right foot, she tried for a new foot hold for her left. It worked; maybe there was a ladder. To be sure she had to move her arms.

"Aha! Oh!" Anna cried. Her left hand struck the wall hard. She found something and held tight. The ladder was there. Anna felt with her right hand and could tell this ladder was different. The steps were attached to the pillar like boards to a tree. There was space for her hands to grasp at the sides but not in the center. She pulled her body closer to the pillar and moved her right arm. It felt stiff. She moved it at the shoulder instead of the elbow.

Anna took a deep breath and then looked down and opened her eyes. If she wanted the flashlight, she had to go down. It looked so far away.

Feeling carefully for each new step; Anna made her way down the shaft. She tried to count the steps, there were at least twice as many as on the first shaft she had come down. The air felt cooler and damp. Anna closed her eyes and continued.

At the bottom of the shaft, with both feet on the floor, Anna looked around, still holding tight to the steps of the ladder with her hands. It took a real effort to let go and turn her back to the ladder. It was the only way she could pick up the flashlight. Her body responded so slowly to her wishes, and her right arm did not want to move at all.

The light was shining toward her. She picked it up with her left hand. First she looked at the ladder, then back up the shaft. It looked long, like it went up forever.

The passageway at this level was twice as wide as the one above. She scanned the walls with the light. The left wall was an uneven cut of stone and dirt. The right was the same solid wood as above. The floor of the passageway was an uneven rock and dirt path. A short distance away it turned to the right. This wasn't the passageway she had seen from the closet in the basement.

Anna took hold of the ladder with her right hand and put her right foot on the first step. She could not hold the flashlight in her hand and grab onto the rungs of the ladder too. She would have to put the flashlight in her jeans as she had done when she first entered the passageway. But then she would have to climb the ladder in the dark.

"Frank, when I get out of here, I'm going to kill you," Anna swore out loud.

She turned and flashed the light down the passageway behind her once more. Not far down it was a corner, and maybe a way out. The light traced the walls, finding where they joined the floor. She started tracing the path back toward her position. There was a small bundle of rags and a half dozen empty wine bottles just a few feet from the ladder. She let go of the ladder and started slowly down the passageway. She stepped over the bundle of rags and continued on. If this led to the closet in the basement, she wouldn't have to climb that ladder in the dark. Descending it had been bad enough.

When she turned the bend and there was a doorway in the wooden wall. The passageway continued straight ahead. Anna checked it with the flashlight. It soon became smaller in both height and width.

Anna turned back to the door. It even had a door handle on it. She was sure it wasn't the entryway to the closet in the basement. Still, it might be a way out. It was a heavy door and Anna had to lean her shoulder against it to open it.

She opened the door and stepped into a small room filled with wine bottles. The door swung closed behind her. The room was narrow, perhaps three times as long as wide. After being in the passageways, it seemed large. Anna reached out; she could not touch both side walls at the same time. Racks of dusty bottles lined the two sides of the room. There were two wooden boxes on the floor, and one was open. On the left side was a narrow stairway. It looked like a ladder braced at the far end of the ceiling. There was no doorway at the end of the ladder.

Anna looked in the first box and saw more bottles. She recalled her father's stories of a bootleg operation in Harrison once. Carefully she stepped over the boxes. There was no door at the other end. She looked back with the flashlight, scanning the ceiling and the walls; no doors at all in sight. Anna sat down on the box.

"Damn you, Frank!" This time she really yelled. In the small dark room the sound of her own voice made her jump. With the light from the flashlight Anna searched the back wall for the doorway through which she had entered. The door had swung into the room but there was no door handle. Without a door handle to pull on she was trapped. The light from the flashlight was growing dimmer. Anna sat down; her back itched and her legs were shaking. She fumbled with the flashlight and almost dropped it.

"If I can't go back and I can't go any further this way. What can I do?" she cried.

She turned off the flashlight for a minute.

The voice was soft. Anna didn't jump but she felt cold, like ice water had crept up the back of her spine. She began to shake.

"Pull that lever down and then retrace your steps, child."

Anna began to shake. She tried to turn on the flashlight. It just shook in her hands. She felt something touch her head, then her hair being pulled. Her head tilted back until she was looking up at the ceiling.

"Pull that lever down and then retrace your steps."

In the darkness Anna reached up with her right hand. The fingers touched a piece of metal, like a pipe. The grip on her hair released. It felt now like a light touch, brushing her hair softly and then not at all. Anna turned the flashlight back on. It was a little brighter. She scanned the racks on the wall and then looked behind her. There was no one there. Anna looked up at the ceiling. Directly above, her right hand was holding tight to a long metal handle. It was the kind appropriate for a barn door. Anna pulled herself up until she was standing on the box. She pushed the handle hard to one side and pushed up. It didn't move.

The light from the flashlight was turning a pale yellow. Anna put the flashlight down on the box and grabbed the handle with both hands. Her foot slipped on the box. She held tight to the handle above until she regained her footing. Something moved. She could feel the air. It wasn't a door above on the ceiling but the wall. The door she had entered swung open halfway. Anna let go of the handle and jumped down. Quickly, she picked up the flashlight and caught the door before it started to swing shut. She had to put one foot against the wall of bottles for leverage to open it all the way.

Back in the passageway Anna hurriedly retraced her steps to the shaft. Her left foot turned sharply and Anna fell against the side of the passageway. She held tight to the flashlight as she landed on the path. She looked back. She had tripped on one of the wine bottles and fallen to her knees. Quickly she scanned the floor of the passageway around her. There were a few empty bottles but the bundle of rags was gone. Anna pushed herself back up on her knees. She looked behind her, only darkness. Anna climbed to her feet and ran to the ladder at the end of the passageway. Before turning out the flashlight and putting it in her pants, she looked back down the passageway. The light was turning a dim yellow. There standing among the wine bottles was the woman clothed in rags. A blanket was pulled over her head and held tightly around her like a robe. Anna could not see her face for it was hidden in the dark.

Anna whirled in her tracks, clicked off the light and shoved the flashlight into the top of her jeans. She started up the ladder as fast as she could go. Her right leg missed a step. Anna caught herself with her arms as she kicked at the wall with both feet. Her right foot found the next higher step on the ladder, but her left wedged between the ladder and the side of the passage.

"Aha! Aaaah! Aaaaaah!" Anna screamed. Each scream was

louder then the one before and with each scream she yanked harder to free her leg.

Finally she jerked her foot loose. Like a cat she climbed up the ladder. Faster and faster she went. Her arms hit a ledge on the side of the shaft. She tried the flashlight and it failed to produce any light at all. Anna felt with her right hand, her left hand holding tight to the ladder. Yes, there was a passageway here. It just didn't seem right. It was too near the bottom of the shaft to be the right place.

They were standing beside the carriage house. Frank had just put the last grave marker back in place.

"She - she haunts the house," Frank said.

"Does she, now?" the priest replied.

"I've seen her."

"Of course, how else could you paint her portrait?"

"The old portrait was damaged."

"She didn't have a necklace in the old portrait, did she?"

"No, she didn't," Frank answered.

"Did you hear that?" Carol interrupted.

"I didn't hear anything," Father David replied.

"Hear what? No, I didn't hear anything," Frank echoed the priest's reply.

"I heard a scream," Carol insisted.

They all stopped and listened for a few minutes. Then Carol Potter and Father David walked over to his car to leave. As he backed the car up to turn around the leave, Carol yelled, "Wait a minute. There it is again."

Again they all listened, but Frank heard nothing.

"I'm going to be late for my appointment tonight or I would like to speak more with you, Frank," the priest acknowledged.

"I'm leaving next week for Seattle," Frank replied.

"Frank, I very much want to talk to you some more before you leave for the army. I am staying at the Jesuit House at Gonzaga. Could you make it for lunch? Let's say Tuesday?"

"Sure, Father; I can do that."

As soon as the car started to move, Frank turned and raced back into the mansion. He ran up the first flight of stairs, cursing the landing which slowed his progress.

As Anna climbed the ladder slowly and more carefully. She felt something touch her foot. Anna shot up the ladder still higher. When she felt a second ledge, she climbed out of the shaft. Again she tried the flashlight; it failed to emit any light at all. Anna clicked it twice, doubting which position was on or off. When it refused to turn on, she wanted to throw it down the shaft. Without light, she was afraid to move. Perhaps this wasn't the way she had come at all.

"Frank, can you hear me?" She listened for a reply. She could hear nothing, but something changed. It wasn't sound, and it wasn't light. It just felt different. It wasn't as cool or damp, and it smelled different. It smelled like fresh air. Feeling about carefully, Anna found the pillar in the passageway at this level and squeezed past it. The darkness was so great, she closed her eyes and continued to step forward. She heard a sound and her eyes opened so wide they hurt; still she could not see. Her pace slowed again as she felt blindly for a ladder, which must be just ahead. Her name, she heard her name. Anna took a few more steps in the darkness and answered.

"Frank! Frank!" She just knew she must be near the entrance.

"Anna, where are you?"

It was Frank's voice. Anna stepped forward cautiously. "I'm coming. I'm coming."

Feeling her way forward in the direction the voice had come Anna continued. She started looking up as she went. She heard his voice again and saw a faint light above at the same time. "Oh! My God! Am I glad to see you!"

Anna repeated the last sentence three times as she climbed up the ladder. The little light above went out as Frank dropped the match and reached down for her.

Anna climbed out of the shaft and into Frank's arms. For a few minutes they just held each other in the dark. Frank slid backwards slowly to get her a safe distance from the shaft.

"Can we get out of here?" Anna said.

"Yes, slide over so I can close the trapdoor."

Frank closed the panel in the floor; then he opened the doors to the closet. Anna crawled out quickly.

Frank followed, and when he caught up with her, put his arms around her and lifted her to the bed. Anna wrapped both her arms tight around him. "No, Frank. No."

He relaxed his arms and felt her pull him closer.

"Frank, just hold me. Hold me."

Frank sat on the edge of the bed and pulled her close in his arms. "My, why are you shaking so?"

"I don't know. I just can't stop. Frank, hold me."

"Are you sure you're all right?" he asked.

Anna nodded yes.

"I'm sorry," Frank said as he pulled her closer in a gentle hug. She pressed her head hard against his chest. She stayed in that position, her arms wrapped tightly around him. She began to shake a little, then to cry. How long she cried he didn't know. He just sat there with Anna curled up on his lap and his arms around her tight.

Chapter 9

The rain stopped just as Frank parked his old truck in the visitor parking near St. Aloysius Church. He started a slow walk onto the campus of Gonzaga University noting the signs at each building. The first pretty coed he met he asked for direction to the Jesuit House.

Father David answered the door when David arrived. "Just a minute; I must get my coat. It may rain again."

Frank walked with Father David to the Bulldog Tavern at the far east end of campus.

"Never have a serious discussion on an empty stomach. They have good beer and burgers here."

Frank studied the posters on the wall of past sports heroes until the waiter brought the beer and burgers to the table. Then Father David raised his glass. "Frank, may God protect you until we meet again."

The cold beer chilled Frank's throat.

"Don't worry, son. We all fear war. I missed the First World War. I went into the seminary. Many of my friends criticized me for that. I don't blame them, they had to serve and a few never returned from Europe."

"That was a different kind of war," David countered.

"All wars are different and the same. The First World War was Mr. Wilson's war, a European dispute that had nothing to do with us. I missed that one but Roosevelt's war caught me. My family was rich, my father's influence far reaching. I volunteered to enter the navy as Chaplain in 1939. Somehow my father managed to have me stationed in what he thought was the safest navel base. Perl Harbor was as far away from the war in Europe as one could get. Then one bloody Sunday the war found me."

David shook his head. "I'm not afraid."

"I was afraid. I lived in fear for four years. My father pulled all the strings he could to get me back home. Then one night a Japanese torpedo found my ship and blew a hole in the bow. God took many that night. The rest of us floated around for two days in those damn little rubber rafts they call lifeboats before being rescued. I was sent back to Pearl until the war ended."

"This war isn't that simple."

"No. This war is different. We as a nation are not threatened. Perl Harbor is in no danger. I pray that there will never be another major war and that we find a better way to settle our differences than by these smaller conflicts."

For a while David ate in silence. He didn't want to get into an argument over the Vietnam War because he had made his decision to serve, not run.

"I am not what I appear," Father David said. "I am a rich man. It is family wealth, a legacy. My father was a banker but more important my grandfather, on my mother's side, owned the bank. We lived in a mansion here in Spokane and Father built that house in Harrison as a summer home."

David smiled. *I bet you don't tell me the real story of those three women he kept in Harrison.*

"I loved going to the lake in the summer. It was so far away from the city and such an interesting place. Harrison was busy then. All those mills along the lakeshore. I loved to ride the steamer too. It was an exciting place. Mining brought the prospect of riches but timber was the real winner. My father was sharper in his dealings with the timber companies than he was in his mining ventures."

Father David stopped while he finished the last of his burger. "Indulge me, David. I will get to the part about the three beautiful French girls shortly."

David blushed.

"My mother died in 1916. After that the house in Harrison became more of a business operation. From the start Father would bring clients down to Harrison on the steamers. They would often travel on to Wallace and the mining districts. But either on the way down or on the return trip they would stay overnight in the house there in Harrison. While Mother was alive it was all strictly business. The year after she died Father kept the house open all winter. I didn't know why until I went down there unannounced in the spring."

Father David finished his beer and set it carefully aside. "I found to my surprise that there were three very beautiful French girls living in the house. I frankly didn't know what to do. My mother's family had already had one fight with my father over my mother's will. If they found out about this, they might fire him as bank president. My father brushed aside my concerns. He had already made plans to remarry, which he hadn't told me. Father assured me that the three women in the house in Harrison would be gone before the summer was over."

Father David stopped his story while the waiter cleared away their dishes.

"I want you to drive me over to the old house. My brother lives there now. There is something I want to show you before I finish this story."

After Father David paid the bill, they walked across the Gonzaga campus to Frank's truck. Following Father David's direction Frank drove across the river and up the south hill where Spokane's elite lived. The house was enormous. It overwhelmed the small lot on which it sat. Frank parked in the driveway in the rear and followed Father David up the back stairs.

They were greeted by a woman in a fire-red dress that contrasted sharply with her hair which was half brown and half grey.

"Frank, this is my sister-in-law Grace." Father David turned toward Frank and said. "Frank here is an artist. I brought him here to show him those old family portraits. Very dull to you and me, but Frank may find them of interest."

Grace sputtered. "Brad just called. Someone hit his car. I've got to drive down to get him."

"Is he hurt?" Father David asked.

"I don't think so. The car was in the parking lot. Brad didn't notice it until he left work."

Grace hurried down the back stairs and Father David led Frank down a long hall to a room in the center of the house. To Frank it looked like a small library. The interior wall on the left was lined with ten evenly hung portraits. Father David stopped at the first one.

"That is James Bradley Marshall IV. He was the first president of the bank. The others are his brothers and their wives. They owned some smaller financial institutions in Montana."

"My brother, half-brother, is James Bradley Marshall V. He even looks like our Father."

Father David walked along the wall looking up at the portraits as he passed. "That is also my grandfather, with my mother, his first wife. As I told you she died in 1916. That's my sister Jane and I in the next picture. I am surprised that Brad keeps that portrait around. This next portrait is the one I wanted you to see."

He pointed at the portrait of the woman with a diamond necklace. "My grandfather gave that necklace to my mother as a wedding present."

Frank swallowed hard. The necklace in the painting was identical to the necklace he had put in Jolie's portrait.

"I can't believe it," Frank said.

"You never found such a necklace when you were cleaning the house in Harrison?"

"Never."

"Then how did you paint it in the portrait of Jolie?"

"I don't know. I just did."

For a few seconds Frank just stood there looking up at the portrait.

"Frank, why did you put the necklace in the portrait of Jolie?"

"I don't know; I just did."

"Why not Doreen's portrait? Or Amiee's?"

Frank turned to face Father David. "Their portraits were all right. All I had to do was a little touch up work. Jolie's was torn; I had to paint a copy."

"And you never saw the diamond necklace?"

"Never. I swear."

Father David put his hand on Frank's shoulder. "Relax Frank. I am not accusing you of lying. It is strange. That blue-diamond necklace was given to Jolie. She was my father's mistress. Jolie died in the fire. The necklace would belong to who ever finds it."

"But I didn't find it."

"Then how did you paint the necklace in Jolie's portrait?"

Frank shook his head. "Maybe she didn't die in the fire. Maybe she haunts that house. I saw her the night I finished that painting."

For a moment Father David was silent. Then in a soft yet serious tone he said, "Don't tell my brother that. Our father dug up my mother's grave to retrieve the jewels she was wearing when she was buried. I fear my brother Brad has the same kind of mind. He is excellent at investing and managing money but absolutely ruthless."

The first day Jolie waited and watched for Frank to return. The second day she went into his room and found his clothes, magazines and books were all gone. The third day she roamed the house using the stairs.

"I am free from the fear of being discovered, yet I miss that boy. He gave me strength."

The fourth day she tried the front door only to find it was locked. Sadly Jolie returned to the passageways and descended to the lowest level.

Anna looked at the postcard; then she turned it over and read the short message again. At least, she knew Frank was now in the army in basic training. A letter would have been nicer. *After all, he isn't the first boy I ever kissed. He wouldn't be the last either. He would be gone two years, probably go to Vietnam. Even when he gets out he would go to Seattle. I don't think I would like it there. Too big. Of course Harrison is too small.*

Anna tossed the postcard aside. "I don't want to live all my life in Harrison. I am not going to have six kids and go nowhere like my mother. That's not for me."

Napoleon raised his head and looked up at Anna.

"College, that's one way out of here," Anna told the dog. Napoleon turned and raced for the door barking.

"I'll get it," Anna yelled. "With Napoleon around no one ever has to ring the doorbell."

Despite her declaration, Jill and Heather ran to the door ahead of her. Napoleon and the two girls raced out the door. When Anna got there, she saw a Jeep station wagon parked along the edge of the road. Napoleon was standing on his hind legs looking in the window at the driver.

"Napoleon! Get down! Now!" Anna scolded the black dog. "Napoleon! Come! Good boy!"

The dog left his find and returned wagging his tail and barking loudly.

"I'm sorry. He just barks. He won't bite," Anna explained. The woman in the driver's seat looked uncertain as she opened the door to get out.

"Stay down! Napoleon! Down!" Anna said sternly.

Napoleon circled the visitor, sniffing her from every direction.

"May I come in?" the woman asked cautiously.

"Oh! Yes! Jill, go tell Mom we have a visitor."

Anna led the way inside. Jill and Heather shadowed the new arrival. Anna's mother met the parade as they entered the small living room.

"Hello! I'm Connie Parker. Most of my friends call me Judge Parker. We just moved into the old house up the hill. What a job! Three old beds and all that old furniture! Well, it's done."

"Pleased to meet you. I'm June Holmes and these are my children. Won't you sit down? Heather, go sit over there."

Anna moved to the doorway of the kitchen as all available seats in the living room were taken by her younger sisters and watched as her mother introduced her children. *Was having six daughters such a great accomplishment or just her mother's only accomplishment?*

"Jill started kindergarten this year. Heather is in second grade. Top of her class! Rose will be ten next month. Janet is in junior high. Elizabeth has started high school and Anna."

"I'm a senior," Anna said.

"Well, then you're the one I really came to see," Connie replied.

Anna wondered what Frank said about her. The woman smiled and continued speaking first to Anna's mother, then to Anna.

"You have such a beautiful family. I bet you're really proud. George and I never had any children. You are so lucky. George was a judge in the county court for fifteen years. When he died, they asked me to serve out the last two years of his term; that's why they call me, Judge Parker. You are so lucky. Well, let me get to the point. I just moved in with my mother. She's only seventy, but she's not spry anymore. I still have many court duties to attend to. In fact, that is the problem; I will have to go to Coeur d'Alene tomorrow. I wondered if Anna could stay with my mother while I'm away? I'll pay of course. Mother doesn't need constant care, but at her age, she shouldn't be left alone."

"I have a job," Anna protested.

"She also has school." Her mother added proudly, "Anna is an honor roll student. She hopes to win a scholarship to college. It's the only way she will ever get there."

"I work every weekend," Anna explained. *And I don't baby-sit old ladies.*

"No problem. I'll be back tomorrow night. Carol, that's my mother, can't get her own dinner. I'll fix her a lunch and leave it in the refrigerator. If you could just check in on her after school and around dinnertime? Would ten dollars be all right?"

Anna shot a quick glance at her mother looking for support. Anna tried to smile and still convey to her mother her feelings. *Don't make me do this. I make more money in tips on any Sunday.*

Mrs. Holmes smiled at Judge Parker and her reply cemented the deal. "I am sure we can work something out. Elizabeth can always help. We can't have her up there alone. Can we, girls?"

The first evening was strange. Anna's fear of being a gopher for a chair-ridden or worst bedridden invalid was quickly erased. Carol, who said she was sixty-something, proved to be very alert. She read books instead of watching TV. She liked music, but played it too loud. As long as it was country western music, Anna didn't complain.

For dinner Anna heated some string beans and rice on the stove and reheated some fried chicken Judge Parker had left in the refrigerator.

"Carol! What would you like to drink?" Anna asked.

"Cognac."

"What?"

"That's a joke," Carol said. "Oh! Water, I guess. I can't drink milk anymore."

"I never had cognac," Anna replied then added, "I had beer though."

"How old are you dear?"

"I'm eighteen."

"Eighteen! That's a good age. You should have had wine by now. In fact, you should know how to drink wine by now. And how to serve it too. Different wines go with different foods. We're having chicken, so a white wine would be served. Ha! I'm dreaming. As sure as Connie is Connie, there is no alcohol in this house."

Anna smiled and opened the cupboards in her search for plates and glasses. *Yes, there is. But it's not up here in the kitchen. What is cognac anyway? Doesn't matter, I am not going back into those tunnels for cognac or even beer.* "Carol, does wine keep?"

"Oh! Yes! Why it's not worth drinking until it's at least three years old. It needs to ferment and age. Gets the acid taste out of it."

"How about a long time? Maybe twenty or thirty years?"

"In a cool wine cellar, it will keep a hundred years. Of course if it gets warm, it will turn to vinegar. Let's eat."

After dinner Carol returned to the living room and tried to make a fire in the fireplace. Anna came to her assistance. *This is why I'm here, to keep you from burning the house down.*

"I love to build fires. Besides you don't want to get splinters."

Anna helped Carol back to her chair, quickly started a fire in the fireplace and then returned to the kitchen. Doing dishes for two was far less of a task then helping with the dishes for eight. Anna consoled herself. When she returned to the living room, she found Carol was reading her French book. "This is interesting. I haven't read anything in French in years?"

"You know French?" Anna said in surprise.

"I was born in France. My father spoke both French and English. My mother spoke only French. I didn't know very much English until I came to this country. I can still read French after all these years!"

The most difficult task that first evening was getting Carol to go to bed. Twice she fell asleep in a chair near the fire. Each time when Anna woke her, she urged her to go upstairs to bed. The third time it worked.

Anna escorted Carol upstairs to her bedroom. The rooms were a little cooler than those downstairs. It was only September but it was time for blankets already.

While Carol changed to her pajamas, Anna faced the question of where she would sleep that night. There was only one other bedroom on the second floor with fresh bedding. That had some things that must belong to Judge Parker, so that room was off bounds. Anna checked the third floor. There were new blankets in one room and none at all in the other. But this was the room with the secret passageway and the room where Frank had slept. *Sleep in his bed! No thanks! I'll sleep on the couch.*

Anna closed the window and went downstairs. She checked on Carol on her way by. The light was out in her room but the door was open. The old woman was already sleeping. Anna left the hall light on in case Carol got up during the night.

When she returned downstairs, Anna added two more logs to the fire. In little over an hour she finished her homework. The love seat was just long enough for her if she curled her feet up a little. What she needed was a pillow and some blankets.

Silently Anna went back up the stairs. When she took the blanket and pillow from Frank's bed, her foot touched something. She pushed the bed sheet aside.

"A crowbar? What is that doing here? Frank, you were a scaredy cat." Anna turned out the light in the third floor bedroom and started down the stairs. She had just reached the hallway on the second floor when she heard it. A loud thud like the slamming of a door. Anna ran down the hall and almost fell down the stairs. She didn't stop until she got to the front door. There she stopped. *I can't leave. What would Mother say? I just can't leave Carol alone.*

Slowly Anna walked back into the living room. She peered in first. There was no one is sight. She looked at the stairway. She listened. The only sound was that of the fire beginning to crackle as the new logs flamed up. Anna walked to the love seat and made a bed for herself. *Why did I ever agree to do this? Damn haunted house.*

She looked up at the portraits on the wall. "You know it's true."

The portrait of Jolie looked back at her and said nothing.

That night just as Anna had nodded off to sleep, Jolie came into the room and stood beside the love seat. The fire had burned low and it no longer hurt her eyes to look at it.

"This is not what I hoped for. He has gone. That strange boy that slept in my bed. He left you. Why?"

Anna did not answer and Jolie moved closer. She put her face down close to the sleeping girl on the couch. Slowly she reached out and touched her cheek. "You are lovely. I know that is a mixed blessing. How strangely you dress for a girl. Some nights I wonder just how many years have past since I was imprisoned here. How long have I been dead?"

Jolie rose to standing position slowly. "It is time for me to leave."

It took a long time before she was able to force the front door to open. It was not locked but it felt so heavy. By the light of the sliver of a moon that hung silently in the sky, Jolie walked across the grass to the carriage house. She paused a moment by the graves and smiled at the new constructed fence around them. "If only I had the strength, I'd reclaim my jewels."

At the road she stopped and looked down at the lights of the city of Harrison. "It has all changed so. I can't. I can't go down there. What if he did return and I was gone. I've lived so long in this prison that it has become my home. I will stay and pray that he will return."

Jolie turned and started slowly back toward the house in Harrison. The door proved even more difficult for her to open to get inside the house. By the time she crossed the living room the fire in the fireplace was but burning embers. Jolie again stopped beside the love seat where Anna lay. "You will get them for me," she whispered. "Listen to me. I know you can hear my voice. Look at the portrait. See those blue diamonds about my neck. Aren't they beautiful? I will help you find them. Remember when you awake, the blue diamond necklace. Look at my portrait when you awake. Look at that necklace. Look carefully, little girl. You must want them to be of use to me."

Chapter 10

The first thing Anna saw when she awoke was the portrait of Jolie looking down from the wall. For a long time she lay there looking back at it. Then Anna quietly took her bedding back upstairs. Carol was still asleep. The bedroom door on the third floor was closed. Anna opened it slowly and after feeling the breeze from the window, she relaxed. "So that was it. Just a door slammed shut by the wind. Guess I'm a real scaredy cat too."

Anna remade the bed and shut the window. All the way back downstairs she repeated, "That's all it was. Just the wind blowing the door shut."

"Scrambled eggs and toast, good enough?" Anna asked when Carol entered the kitchen almost a half-hour later.

"Cocoa. I like my cocoa," Carol replied.

Anna filled the tea pot and searched the cabinet for the cocoa. For herself she poured a glass of juice. This job wasn't going to be as hard as Anna thought it would. Carol was pretty self-sufficient.

At the welcome sound of Napoleon's barking, Anna hurried to the door to find the big black dog on the porch and Elizabeth just starting up the steps.

"Hi! You up?" Elizabeth asked.

"Of course, I'm up. Come on in. No! Napoleon! Stay!"

Elizabeth hurried in and went straight to the kitchen. "Hi! My friends call me Lisbeth but my name is really Elizabeth."

"Well, my real name is Dorene Carol Laponce Potter. Ain't that a mouthful. Just call me Carol. Glad to meet you Lisbeth. Do you want some cocoa?"

Carol moved slowly but efficiently. She finished fixing her cocoa and a cup for Elizabeth. Anna took advantage of Elizabeth's presence to make a quick exit to the bathroom. She would need to leave for school soon.

Carol took charge of the dishes after breakfast. The dangers Anna decided were from her doing too much. Starting a fire in the fireplace wasn't beyond her but it was dangerous, so was every trip up those stairs. As Anna and Elizabeth were leaving Anna paused before the portrait of Jolie. "See that necklace. Doesn't it look real?"

"I bet it is worth a lot of money," Elizabeth said.

"It certainly is," Carol said from across the room. "Now get going or you'll miss that school bus."

Without a sound the trapdoor in the closet to Carol's room open. Jolie climbed up into the closet and listened. She could hear the new voice downstairs. Another young voice, perhaps one of Anna's many sisters. "Now is my chance. That old woman won't come up those stairs unless she has to. Stay in my house, will you; well there is a price."

Jolie moved silently to the closet. She looked over the dresses and took one out into the room and laid it on the bed. "Nice but too bright. I had best select a darker color that will not be easily seen in the dark of night."

One by one she examined all the dresses in the closet. None suited her. "I have worn these rags long enough. There must be something here."

Jolie looked through the dresser. In the very bottom drawer she found what she wanted. "Ah! How appropriate! A black negligee. What use would an old woman have for this? A little large but it will have to do."

At the sound of the front door slamming Jolie moved quickly to the window. She watched Anna and Elizabeth hurry down the road. "No need to worry. That old woman will likely stay down stairs all morning."

Jolie changed clothes, listening all the while for the sound of footsteps. She left her old rags in the trunk at the foot of the bed and returned to the closet and slipped back into the passageway. Through the dot size holes in the wall she watched as Carol finished her cocoa and then start upstairs. Jolie hurried through the passageways to follow the old woman's movements. She did not stop at her room on the second floor but continued although slowly up to the third floor.

As fast as she could travel through the narrow passageways Jolie made her way to the third floor. By the time she entered the closet in what was once her bedroom, Jolie could hear Carol.

Jolie knelt and peeked out between the crack between the closet doors. "What are you doing in my room, old woman?"

Carol was seated at the small secretary desk. Jolie opened the closet door just a crack. *The boy who was here this summer searched that desk and did not find its secret; neither will you.*

Jolie watched as Carol opened the small ornate drawer on the right. Then slipping her small hand inside, she pushed up on the wood above the drawer. The side of the desk opened revealing a chamber about the size of a coffee cup. Carol reached inside the chamber and then exclaimed, "A diary! Where is the necklace? It had to be here."

Jolie put one hand on the doorknob inside the closet and with the other she grasped her dagger. "I will kill you. No one steals from Jolie."

Jolie opened wide the door to the closet but she hesitated. *If I kill you the girl will leave too. I need that girl.*

In silence Jolie silently closed the closet door. With a burst of anger, Carol opened the remaining two drawers in the desk. Finding nothing of value she searched the trunk at the foot of the bed. She stopped to rest before she began to systematically search the entire room. She even looked under the mattress. The only jewelry she found was a pair of earrings in the top drawer to the dresser.

Carol paused; her search had come to its end. She went to the window and looked out. "I can't believe that my own grandson is a thief. I bet he didn't take it with him. No. More likely Frank hid them somewhere here in the house."

Jolie listened at the closet door. "Old woman, you escaped death today. Had you opened this door I would have killed you."

Jolie opened the trapdoor in the closet and slipped down into the passageway. She heard the clicking of the door handle being turned in the closet door. "So you will finally search the closet. You will find nothing here."

Jolie pulled the trapdoor closed and stood in the darkness. "Things have changed. When that boy first came to this house and set me free, I could hardly see in the bright light. Now I have become accustomed to it. In this darkness I need not see at all for I know every splinter in this prison."

As she stepped along in the dark Jolie pondered. *The old woman did not hear me speak but she is old, perhaps hard of hearing. If she had opened the closet door sooner would she have seen me? If so I would have had to kill her. How did she know about my necklace? She has my diary now, but that will not lead her to where my blue-diamond necklace is hidden. The girl, Anna is the key. Only she can help me get back what is mine.*

Anna encouraged her sisters to come to the house. Elizabeth's unannounced visit to the mansion was followed the next day by Janet and Jill. Carol was delighted to have company. She even welcomed Napoleon into the house when Judge Parker was not home.

The month of September passed without Anna receiving a letter or even another postcard from Frank. It was not until late October that Anna got a letter from him saying he was in Texas in infantry school. He complained about the hot humid weather and ended with, "As soon as we finish here we will be shipping out so there is no sense in writing me at this address."

"Who said I was going to write you anyway," Anna pouted. "I have plenty of boyfriends. Bet I know where they will ship you."

By now Anna was staying with Carol two nights a week. She had even moved to the third floor bedroom, Frank's room. First she had hung a cross on the wall by the bed. Her mother called it a Celtic cross because it had a circle behind it. "A ghost? No. There is no ghost in this house. I should never have gone down into that passageway. I just scared myself, but how did Frank paint that necklace in Jolie's portrait? It must be here somewhere."

Carol always appeared very glad to have Anna come stay with her and encouraged her to come even when Judge Parker was home. Anna too liked the arrangement. The house was the only place where

Anna had a room of her own. Neither Judge Parker nor Carol ever came up to the third floor. At night when she climbed the stairs to the third floor she would say, "The more I study the better my grades. That's why I'm here instead of out having fun with the other kids in class."

When she undressed for bed at night Anna sometimes danced around the room. *I wish this house were mine. What a joy to live in such a big house with fine furniture and of course a man too.* "This is my room now, Frank. Oh! You still want to come in?"

She would stop and pause at the window just before climbing into bed. *I wish all my sisters could be here. Well, maybe Elisabeth will be here next year when I go off to college. All A's this year. I have to get out of Harrison. This is my study. My own room, something I don't have at home.*

Each night Anna not only did her homework; she studied the next chapter in each of her books.

"What are you studying tonight?" Carol asked Anna one night after dinner.

"Just homework. Teachers think we don't have a life. They really pour on the homework. But I have to do it. If I'm to get out of Harrison, I need a scholarship."

"Maybe I can help, dear."

Carol helped Anna with her math. She also read her themes and history reports. Unlike her mother, Carol did not have a dozen other things to do. The more Anna let her help, the happier Carol seemed.

Late one night when Connie was in Coeur d'Alene and Anna was sitting on the love seat in the living room looking up at the portrait of Jolie, Carol came down the stairs. "Are you still up? I just can't sleep tonight."

"Me neither," Anna replied.

"What's the matter, child? You burn out?"

"I can't be burned out. I'm only eighteen. That's for old folks."

Carol sat down in the chair between the love seat and the fire. "Whose portrait are you staring at?"

"Jolie."

"Don't you like Dorene or Amiee?"

"She seems special." Anna glanced at Carol, then back at the portrait of Dorene. *I bet you liked the blonde. She's your type. Well, Jolie is mine.*

"Is it the necklace or the look in her eyes?" Carol asked.

"I posed for that painting," Anna replied.

"Did you really?" Carol asked. "Frank told me he based it on an old painting he found in the house."

"He did. But he had trouble. The painting was torn, so I posed for him."

"Where did you get the necklace?"

Anna turned toward Carol. The old woman was studying her carefully, like her mother did when Anna came home late from a date. "You'll have to ask Frank."

"Don't sass me, girl. I know you don't have it. You work like a demon trying to get straight A's. If you had that necklace, it would buy a college education and a lot more."

Anna looked back up at the portrait. So the necklace was real, worth thousands of dollars. "I bet it's in her grave. Every day when I pass that grave, I get the chills. It must be there."

Carol shook her head slowly.

"Why not?" Anna said.

"Now think about it. Frank is the key, not the grave. You didn't see the necklace in the old portrait did you?"

"I don't remember it." Anna thought a moment. "No, I'm sure it wasn't. I didn't like the painting. Frank made such a fuss over her. Over his Jolie."

"The point is, Anna, if the necklace was in the grave, Frank would have had to dig it to know what it looked like."

"Frank would never do that."

"You like Frank don't you?" Carol's voice became softer until it was almost a whisper. "I think that is why I can't sleep tonight. He's over there. He's in danger. I feel he's been hurt. I don't know why I just feel it."

A flash of heat crossed Anna's face. *How dare you? He is not your boyfriend. You're only his grandmother. If something is wrong, I would know, not you.*

Carol bowed her head and bit her lower lip. The look on her face was sad, almost as if she was reading Anna's thoughts.

Anna rose from the love seat and started for the stairs. She felt guilty even if the old lady couldn't really know what she was thinking. She was his grandmother, and she was concerned. "Don't worry. He's all right. I'll go get the letters he wrote me."

Anna brought the last three letters she had received from Frank. Carol read then aloud that night.

Letters from Vietnam came less often to Anna as the winter snows turned to spring rains. The gloomy outlook continued when Anna failed to win any scholarships to college. And when she brought home all the papers on school loans her father just shook his head slowly. The rains continued into the early summer when Anna worked in the bar instead of the café for a while. One night her father came in and watched for a while and then left without ordering anything. The next morning her mother talked to Anna about going back to being a waitress at the café.

Anna changed jobs but she also began spending more time at the mansion away from her father. At night after work Anna would talk to Carol about running away from Harrison.

"Don't despair, child. Frank will return," Carol assured her.

From behind the wall near the fireplace Jolie bristled. "It is your fault, old woman. By now I would have persuaded her to dig up that grave. No, you had to tell her the necklace wasn't in the first portrait. You spoiled my plan. Without you around I would have succeeded. If I am to remain imprisoned here I will have my jewels too."

"What did you say?" Carol asked.

"I'll never leave Harrison," Anna replied.

"No, after that, About being imprisoned here?"

"I didn't say that, but it's true. I am a prisoner in Harrison."

"Interesting," Carol replied. She nodded her head slowly and then asked, "You got an A in French?"

"Lot of good that did me," Anna retorted. "I didn't get a scholarship."

"You know, Anna. Those books are in French too." Carol pointed to the old books in the small bookcase near the portraits. "The women in those portraits are French. Their names are French, Amiee, Dorene, and Jolie, but there are no last names. Connie wants to take the portraits down. Not our family, she says. I like them, don't you?"

"Frank painted a portrait of me," Anna replied. *I haven't heard from that rat for over a month. He'd better be staying out of trouble.* Anna looked up at the portrait of Jolie.

"Connie is going to see the previous owners, or more correctly his descendants to see if they want the paintings. Father David said we could keep them but that wasn't good enough for Judge-know-it-all. Father David will not tell her what he knows about the women in the pictures. Why do you think he is so secretive?"

Anna turned on the love seat and pulled her legs up until her head rested on her chin. "Frank said that they didn't look enough alike to be sisters."

"Sisters! No. There is a family resemblance for here in Harrison. What if they were mistresses? None of them ever married a Marshall. That is what I think troubles that Father David."

"Carol! Come on! How can a man have three mistresses?"

The old woman leaned her head back against the chair and closed her eyes for a moment. "No, one man could. I wonder what the other Mr. Marshall, Father David's brother, will tell Connie?"

"Somebody's grandmother, that's what he will say. One of them might have been the mistress of the house in the sense of being the woman in charge, but only in that sense of the word."

Carol nodded her head and smiled. "She might be both. I'll bet it will turn out that Jolie was the mistress of the house. She was also probably the favorite of the man who owned it. All three women were here for the same reason. Men of power often demand that women be available to them wherever they go. These men were rich enough to arrange it. And the poor girls were foolish enough to do it."

Anna looked up at the three portraits and shook her head. Carol was saying what she and Elizabeth had said when they first saw the paintings. Still Anna did not want to believe it. She felt she had to defend the women in the portraits. After all, she posed for Jolie's portrait. "I am shocked at you, Carol. She doesn't look at all like that kind of a girl."

"What do you think they looked like? Pretty? Yes. Young and poor? You bet. The first winter we came to western America I would have sold myself for a good meal. We were cold and hungry all the time. The rain and snow came right through the roof. Where we lived in Montana, we didn't even have panes in the windows. Damn, it was cold. When we moved to Helena things were different. Too many had gotten there before us. Believe me. It was a desperate time."

Anna hugged her knees. *So you were poor when you came to this country. Does that give you the right to make up stories about someone else?* "I bet she's someone's grandmother. Even if she's not, you shouldn't talk about her like that. She and I have something in common."

"Now who's talking nonsense?"

Anna put her feet back down to the floor and tossed back her shoulders. "She has my profile. My nose."

"She's your size all right."

"How do you know that?"

Carol sat up straight and looked over at Anna. "Honey, you are sitting in the same love seat. You look just the same as she does."

Anna sat there. She looked at the painting and adjusted her position, turning her head toward the fire.

"Look like sisters. She was just your height. Narrow waist too. Tell me, Anna, why did you come to her defense just now?"

"I don't know. I like her, I guess."

Carol beamed. "Want to know more about her?"

"Yes, I would. She's dead. Maybe Judge Parker will find out something and not what you think."

Carol's eyes had a twinkle to them. "I found her diary. I put it upstairs in my bedroom. It's interesting reading, shocking at times.

You know enough French to read it. I'll let you have it when I am finished."

Anna looked up at the portrait, then back at Carol. "A diary! Jolie's diary?"

That night when she went up to bed, Carol showed Anna the diary. It was the same shape and color of her French dictionary but thinner. Anna carefully opened it to the first page. There in elegant but large hand writing was JOLIE ELISABETH DESCARTES.

"It is a diary!"

"Anna, of course it is. You know it starts when Jolie is only sixteen. She turned sixteen the day she left France for England."

Anna said nothing but reached out and touched the book with her right hand. *Sixteen! She was only sixteen. How old was she when she lived here in Harrison?*

Anna took a flashlight up to the third floor with her that night. After she was sure that Carol was asleep, she entered the closet. It took a few twists of the door handle before she could open the trapdoor. She didn't go down into the passageway. For a moment she stared at the darkness. She closed her eyes. What she could see was what she remembered. *Is someone down there? Did I really see her? Was it Jolie? No. It was all an allusion. I was scared. Who wouldn't be? It was all Frank's fault, he made me go down there. I made it all the way to the bottom and back.*

Slowly she closed the trapdoor. Anna walked over to the bed and turned off the light. "Jolie could have gone down there. Frank was right. This was her room. I just know it. Jolie, are you really down there? Are you hiding something? How did Frank know about that necklace? He must have found it. I bet he didn't take it with him. There is nothing else for me to do. No college. No Frank. No way out. Another year in Harrison. I'm going to find your necklace. You don't mind, do you?"

Standing in silence just beyond the trapdoor Jolie nodded. "I will help you find it but then I will take it from you, for it is mine."

Chapter 11

Anna knelt by the fireplace and poked the last log a little farther back onto the embers. For a moment she wished Frank were there sharing the warmth of the fire with her. Cool evenings in October had been replaced by cold ones is November. Was it cold where he was? Was he still in Vietnam? Anna watched the sparks fly up the chimney.

Snow hadn't come yet to Harrison, but freezing rain had. Connie had canceled her trip to Coeur d'Alene this week. Still Anna came each night to the old mansion. She did so to read, she told them, and they didn't question it. Carol welcomed her visits. She was especially happy when Anna brought one of her little sisters with her.

Connie had returned from a trip to Spokane. She brought with her a new robe and lightweight black and red blanket for Carol. After dinner that night they all sat around the fireplace and Connie began to tell of her visit to the Marshalls' house in Spokane.

"Brad Marshall looks something like Father David, but he doesn't act like him at all. At first he was somewhat reserved. Rich people usually are. He may have been concerned that I was a judge. After a while he let his guard down and I got the whole story though I don't know if any of it is true. Rich people tend to remember the grand things in history and link some relative to each event. They all had relatives who were generals or admirals in the war, never just soldiers or sailors, if you believe the stories."

Anna pushed back from the fire.

"Get on with the story," Carol insisted. "What did he say? They aren't his relatives, are they? I knew they were not."

"Father David is his half-brother and I got the impression he wasn't a favorite of the family."

"I don't mean him. The three women?" Carol cried.

"I'll get to that. Brad Marshall began to tell me how his father, James Bradley Marshall IV, came to Spokane before the big gold rush. He came after he had already made a bundle in Montana and formed a bank in Spokane to finance the development of the mining claims in north Idaho. Gold and placer mining didn't last very long. The moment the miners switched to silver and began to sink shafts and ship the ore out to be milled, they needed capital. He also backed the sawmills that sprang up everywhere. The big timber companies got exclusive contracts to supply timber to the bigger mining claims. Bradley Marshall backed a few smaller mills that were then free to sell timbers to all the smaller mining companies. This house wasn't built until 1912 just after the big fire. Wallace made a big thing of rebuilding with bricks, but that was just the business section of town. The homes were rebuilt with wood. James Bradley Marshall IV made another fortune."

"Connie, dear," Carol interrupted. "Did this Bradley Marshall build this house? Did he live here? In Harrison?"

"Wait, Mother! I'll get to that. He didn't exactly say his father built this house. He said his father financed the construction of the house. He told me the house belonged to his brother and he himself had never been here. He assured me that Father David would not leave any family portraits in the house."

"Not relatives," Carol repeated. "See! I told you."

"Mother!" Connie said in her official voice. "Let me tell the story. This house was, according to Brad Marshall, a family retreat for his father's first wife. After the fire in 1917, they never came back to Harrison. He guessed that it also served as a rest place when his father had to travel to Wallace or one of the other mining towns. His father told of taking investors up to the mining area in the winter. They would travel to Coeur d'Alene on Corbin's electric train. From Coeur d'Alene they would take the steamboat to Harrison and go upriver to Cataldo in a smaller boat. Then they would take Corbin's narrow-gage railroad on up to Kellogg or Wallace. It was quite a long journey, especially in bad weather. So they would stay overnight in Harrison and continue their travel the next day."

Carol giggled.

Connie glared at her.

Carol turned to Anna and said, "Now there was a very nice hotel down on Main Street. Elegant place. Why would they come all the way up here to stay? Three charming girls? French too! What a clever way to encourage one to invest in silver mining."

"I don't believe it," Anna said quickly.

"There is a wicked twist to the story," Connie said, raising her voice to quiet the room. "I really shot a hole in Marshall's story - by accident. I asked if he had a picture of his father. Of course, he did. He took me into the study where the whole wall was lined with family portraits, not photographs. I didn't think even rich people did that anymore. There was James Bradley Marshall IV. He had three brothers. Believe it or not, one was a dwarf. Anyway, he went on to tell me what great things each had done. Then I did it. I had just heard too much of how great these old men had been. Without them, there wouldn't have been any industry in north Idaho at all."

"Connie, get to the point," Carol pleaded. "You can be so abrupt when you want to."

"OK! There were two paintings of his father. In one he was with a woman and one small boy. In the other he was with a different woman and two children. I asked him which of the women was his mother. The first he said was David and his mother. She died and his father remarried. Brad's mother was in the second picture with him and his sister. That's when I shocked him. I said, 'Well, Mr. Marshall, you should come to Harrison. In one of the paintings I was telling you about there is a necklace just like that one his first wife is wearing.'"

"Connie!"

"Mother, don't interrupt. Let me tell you this Mr. Marshall was really taken back. He assured me I was mistaken. Then he suddenly remembered another appointment and my visit was over."

Carol shook her head slowly. "You shouldn't have told him about the necklace."

Anna stared at the portrait. "Was she his wife or his mistress? She wasn't just a prostitute?"

"Prostitutes don't wear diamond necklaces," Connie assured her. "But I can tell you this. She doesn't look like the woman in the painting, the first Mrs. J. B. Marshall. Father David wouldn't tell me the story; neither did his brother Brad Marshall. We may never know the whole story. Perhaps even they don't know. Anyway the paintings should come down."

"Oh!" Anna said in protest.

"Now, Connie. It's my house. I say keep them where they are until you get some new paintings to replace them. Frank had a few that I liked. We will wait until he returns."

"Mother, if someone came to visit, who would you say they are? Not our relatives! Please!"

"They are the people who used to live here. Their graves are out there by the carriage house. I insist they stay right where they are at least until Frank returns."

"There are three graves and three women," Anna added, not quite sure why she, too, wanted the portraits to stay.

"I forgot about that. I told Brad Marshall there was a graveyard. He didn't seem to care, unlike Father David, who was concerned we might choose to move the graves."

"I wish Frank were here," Carol said. "He was clever. He would understand what we have here. I am very disappointed with you, Connie. You should never have told him about the portrait. You're too self-righteous. Being a judge did that to you."

"It's your house, but when Frank gets back from Vietnam I want him to paint us some new pictures to hang on that wall." Connie pounded her fist on the table as if to signal the meeting adjourned.

Anna returned to her room on the third floor. She picked up Frank's last letter and then decided not to read it again. "We don't have to wait for Frank to return."

She picked up Jolie's diary and sat on the bed to read. After a reading a few pages she left her bed and dug out her old note cards of French and English words. She would brush up on her French. The diary was not as simple to read as she had thought it would be.

On the first card was UNIVERSITÉ; on the flip side UNIVERSITY. WINE and VIN, WINE CELLAR, CAVE.

"Let's change the subject." She looked up LOVER, AMOUREUX.

"Damn, Frank! Why don't you write?"

A few more words and she put the cards aside. Nothing she had heard tonight shed any light on the secret passageways in the house. Connie didn't know they existed. She also didn't know about the diary. For some reason Carol had never told her. Maybe she was waiting for Anna to finish reading it.

Anna sat back and again began to struggle with the diary. In a few hours she had read enough of it to begin to picture Jolie in her mind.

The book began with Jolie's sixteenth birthday. The first few pages told of leaving France. Her parents had both been killed when the Germans had captured the town where she lived. The French managed only to destroy her home in their attempts to recapture it.

Jolie's first goal was to get as far away from the war in Europe as she could. She and her two cousins had bribed a fisherman to take them to England. When the English required that they go on to America where Jolie had relatives or return to France, they chose America. Jolie expected to find modern cities here in the west with lots of rich men and few women. Anna knew enough history of Idaho to guess what Jolie found was a great disappointment.

The three girls spent one winter with Jolie's uncle who lived ten miles west of Missoula and sold supplies to the nearby logging camps. When the loggers got paid, they would come down to his cabin.

"All I ask is half of what they give you," he told Jolie. "That's generous of me, for I give you my house and my food."

That spring Jolie took her two cousins and moved on to Helena. A year later they moved to Spokane. At that time, Jolie was still younger than Anna, but far more experienced with men. She set a high price for her favors and demanded Amiee and Dorene do the same. Jolie became the mistress of the house in Harrison when she was just eighteen.

Anna put her head in her hands for a moment. *No wonder Carol said the things she did. It's all here in the diary. Amiee, Dorene and Jolie were cousins. They were brought here as kept women. It was only a step above living in a bordello. Carol was defending them when she told of how desperate she was when her family first came to this country.* "I bet Carol is right, that Mr. Marshall doesn't know as much about Jolie as we do. But Carol doesn't know about the passageway. I know and Frank knows. But Frank never went down there. He doesn't know where the passage goes."

She walked to the closet. She had a flashlight. "I'm not afraid. Jolie was a girl just like me. Now she is dead. I saw the grave. I can go down there. I know about the shaft so I won't fall and this time I have good batteries in my flashlight. I must be careful not to get lost again. I wonder? Could the necklace be hidden down there? No, Frank could never go down there. Still I bet something is hidden down there."

Anna opened the trapdoor and looked down. Then she let it bang shut, opened the closet door and returned to the bed.

Jolie stood quietly in the shadows in one of the empty bedrooms on the second floor. She watched as Anna started up the stairs to the third floor. After Connie and Carol had gone to their rooms, Jolie moved silently out into the hall. She listened at the doorway for a long time before she entered the room where Carol slept.

"You are too curious," Jolie whispered. She raised her silver dagger above Carol's neck. "If they listen to you, they will all soon be searching for my jewels."

Carol turned her head on the large bolster pillows on her bed, still deep in sleep.

Jolie stepped back from the bed.

Carol was now facing the ceiling.

Jolie again positioned the dagger just above the throat. Then she looked at the face again for any sign her victim might awake. Slowly she lowered the dagger to her side.

"I cannot do it. I would kill you now but that would only bring more people to search my house," Jolie whispered.

For a few minutes Jolie just stood by the bed. "You know, old woman, you remind me of my cousin Dorene. She used to sleep here. Like you, she would prop her head up on several pillows. For Dorene's memory I let you live. But you must not persist in probing the secrets of this house. Let it be. What is in it for you? Like your daughter, Connie, you should be condemning us, not defending us."

When Jolie turned to leave, she saw the new black and red blanket on the trunk at the foot of Dorene's bed. She picked it up and wrapped it around her like a cloak. "You don't need this. I wonder how soundly you would sleep if you knew that I killed a man in this very room?"

A noise from the room above startled Jolie. She looked up and said, "What is that girl doing now?"

Anna took a dozen note cards and a pencil with her when she returned to the closet.

The first card she labeled JOLIE'S ROOM. This she placed at eye level in the passageway just below the trapdoor. She made her way toward the center of the house. She wrote SHAFT on a card, erased it, and wrote PUITS. She wedged the card between two boards in the wall just before the pillar. After she slipped around the pillar, she left a note-card PREMIER ÉTAGE on the ladder.

"French is strange. The third floor is the second floor above the ground floor. If I were still in school, I'd get extra class credit for this." The sound of her own voice seemed a higher pitch in the narrow passageway.

Anna started down. The passageway was much warmer as she descended. Anna stopped every ten steps of the ladder and left a card. In so doing she discovered two landings she had passed in the dark the first time in the passageway. She left a card at each floor. She entered the second landing. After a few steps she came to a door. Anna opened it a little and peeked inside.

"A chair? Oh!"

She stepped inside and turned the handle on the closet door. This was the basement closet where she had changed clothes when Frank did her portrait. The door handle worked just as the one in Jolie's closet did. She remembered now that one side of the closet opened into the passageway instead of having a trapdoor.

In three nights Anna had mapped the passageways on all but the lowest level. She had listened and watched Carol and Connie in the living room from a hidden chamber behind the wall near the fireplace. She had found another behind the painting on the other wall. To get between the two chambers Anna had to crawl on hands and knees in a tunnel under the floor. She had planned to reach the wine cellar, but her memory of the last visit to that area was veiled in fear. No matter how many times she told herself Jolie was dead and buried, she still remembered someone in the lowest level of the passageway. Each time she entered into the secret passageways Anna told herself, "The first time I came down into these passageways I remember ending up in a wine cellar. What happened after that? I know I did find my way out. Frank was waiting for me. I do remember that. The wine cellar must be on that lowest level, lower than the basement. I will not go there tonight. I'll wait for Frank to return."

Chapter 12

Frank felt with his hand in the warm muddy water.

"Keep looking. We need that radio," Sergeant Jackson ordered.

"Got it." Frank held the radio up in his right hand. The six other men in the rice paddy stood up and started sloshing their way in the dark grey light back to the trail. Frank searched with his left hand until he found the webbed-belt. Then he dragged the remains of Private Williams out of the water. He had been the clown of the squad until a few minutes ago when he stepped on that mine.

Sergeant Jackson handed the radio to the soldier standing beside him and pointed up the trail.

"What of Williams?" Frank asked.

"We have to keep moving. They will be shelling this area at 2030."

"I can carry him," Frank replied.

"OK. Potter and Ram rear guard and stay close. We can't wait for you. Charlie is right behind us. That mine not only cost us time; now Charlie knows just where we are."

Frank scanned the area before him trying to separate the low mist from the shadows of the jungle just beyond the rice paddies. Letting the corpse of private Williams slip slowly to the wet ground, Frank squatted in the tall grass and again scanned the edge of the water, this time through the sights of his M-16. A hundred Charlies could be hiding out there. But none moved out of the impenetrable darkness of the jungle when the squad move departed.

"Let's go," Ram whispered.

"Not yet," Frank replied.

A grey veil of rain began to advance across the rice paddy. Frank noticed another movement as he slowly moved his head from right to left, then back again. The edge of the rice paddy parted. The dark shadow of the jungle advanced. First it was just one, then two, then a dozen Vietcong soldiers silently crossing the rice paddies. Instinctively Frank set his sights on the shadow to his right; Ram would take the left side. Their path of fire would meet in the middle.

This was not time for a rifle to jam or a single shot to miss its target. They were outnumbered six to one; the rest of the squad would not be coming back. This is what the rear guard was for, stopping any enemy soldier who might follow. For a second Frank wished he had given the letters in his pack to one of the other men to mail if he did not catch up with them. It was too late for that now.

It was snow not rain that fell in north Idaho that same night. More snow the next morning had closed the roads leaving Harrison. No one came to the café, not even the locals, so that afternoon Anna walked back up the hill, first home, then on to the mansion. Carol was in the living room reading by the fireplace.

"Nice night for a brandy and coffee."

"Sorry, Carol. Want me to fix some hot chocolate?" Anna asked.

"No. I just wish Connie were not so strict. I'm not a child."

Anna went down to the basement and paced the floor. The wine cellar was under this floor; she was sure of that. With a bar down here it was logical to have an entrance to the wine cellar too. It wasn't through the closet. Anna looked behind and under the bar. No trapdoor in sight.

"Strange place! Isn't it?"

Anna jumped at the voice behind her. Carol walked so slowly on stairways that silence was a natural partner.

"I bet you're snooping around trying to find out where they hid the liquor? Don't blame you, honey; with weather like this, one could use a drink. It would warm our spirits. I bet they left some liquor behind. The problem is where."

"Perhaps they kept it behind the bar. There is lots of shelf space here," Anna suggested.

Carol made her way slowly across the room to the bar.

"No! It should be right here." Carol pointed to the floor under the bar. "The Marshalls were rich. Rich people entertain; that calls for wine. To keep wine you need a cellar. It also becomes a good place to put the rest of the liquor."

Anna opened one of the closet doors and looked at the lattice structure inside. "I saw a movie once where they had bottles in little holes like these."

"Wine bottles. You store wine on its side. That keeps the cork wet," Carol told her. "Only the rich drank wine, but the Marshalls were rich."

"Idaho had prohibition so they had to hide it," Anna countered.

"No. This place was built in 1912; prohibition didn't come until 1917."

"The year of the fire," Anna said. She pounded on the wall behind the bar. "It doesn't sound hollow. But it is wood. Could it just be thick wood?"

Carol walked over past the fireplace. "Why not under the floor? Say, right there where the bar is now?"

"Oh, no! How would you get in?" Anna shook her head. "Something isn't right. I can't understand why anyone would have a bar in the basement anyway. How did they ever get it down here?"

"See that outside door down there? They brought it down those steps and slid it across the floor to here." Carol pointed to the floor where the bar stood. "The wine cellar should be here."

"But why put it under the bar?"

"Perhaps the bar has been moved."

Anna studied the floor by tapping it with her heel on a few boards. They sounded solid. Thick wood floor panels would sound the same.

"How do you know the wine cellar is under the bar?" Anna asked.

Carol was silent for a moment before replying, "I read it in Jolie's diary."

Anna walked over to the bar and pushed on one end. Carol watched a minute and then joined her. Together they pushed the bar out a foot farther away from the wall. The other end refused to budge. With a lot of effort on Anna's part, they rotated one end of the bar another four feet away from the wall. There, under the bar, the wood was darker than the rest of the floor. In the center of the darkened wood was a trapdoor. It even had a notch in the edge for a handle. Anna lifted the door and peered down into the wine cellar below. "Oh! My God!"

Anna stepped back from the entrance. She hadn't dreamed it. She had been there. She felt for a moment the chill of fear she had felt when she had been trapped there in the dark. Someone had told her the way out, more correctly the way back to the secret passageways. It was right there behind that wall. Anna jumped just as she had that day when someone had touched her in the dark. It had really happened. She looked around the basement room.

"What's wrong, dear?" Carol asked.

"How long can you live with only wine to drink?"

Carol didn't answer. She started for the narrow stairway.

"Carol! Stop. You could fall. Let me do that." Anna climbed down the narrow steps using the racks in the wall for support. She wiped the dust off the labels and read a few names on the bottles. Carol instructed her to bring up a bottle of cognac and one of champagne, saying if anything was still good it would be these.

That night Anna tasted her first champagne and Carol told her a story. It was about a Christmas that happened long ago at her home in Lens, before she left France. Anna listened and tried to picture Carol as a young girl. She laughed when Carol slipped and spoke a while in French and then switched back to English as if she hadn't noticed she had done so. A little champagne had relaxed them both.

After Anna had helped Carol get ready for bed, she carried the last of the champagne upstairs to her own room on the third floor. Jolie's diary was on the bed. Anna picked it up and quickly opened it. She remembered that name, yes, it was there. Jolie too lived just outside the town of Lens in France.

For a while Anna read the beginning of the diary again. Jolie had been a young girl, just like Anna. She had come from a large family. Unlike Anna, Jolie had many brothers but not sisters. Early in the First World War she had lost all her family.

Anna finished the bottle of champagne and shut the diary with a bang.

"It can't happen. She can't have hidden in the house for fifty years," Anna proclaimed. "I'll prove it."

She took her flashlight and went down into the wine cellar. She pulled the trapdoor closed over her head. Then, standing on one of the boxes of wine, she pulled straight down on the lever above her. The secret door to the passageway swung open.

Anna proceeded slowly. She knew that the house was set on the edge of a rock outcropping. She found the tunnel along the face of the rock. This she reasoned must be the base level of the passageways throughout the house. She had been here before. With the narrow beam of light she located the ladder leading up to the rest of the house. Between her and the ladder were the blanket and the wine bottles. Anna remembered these and stooped to picked up the bottles and carefully set then aside.

"No wonder I was scared. This place is really spooky." Anna knelt down and pulled the top of the blanket aside. The mummified remains of a woman with long dark hair looked back at her. Anna turned the flashlight away. For a long time she knelt there as if frozen in place. She tried to pray and could not find the words. She started to shake, to cry. She dropped the flashlight. Slowly she pulled the blanket back over the corpse.

"Who are you?" Anna whispered.

"Je m'appelle Jolie."

Anna picked up the flashlight and sat back on her legs. The corpse had not moved, surely it had not spoken and yet she heard a voice. She answered. "Jolie! No! You can't be. You're dead. I mean you're buried in the graveyard. You can't be here."

"Comment tu, t'appelles?"

For a moment Anna could not answer. *That voice - I have heard it once before. This time like before it comes from behind me. It is not this corpse but someone in the passageway with me.* "I am Anna. Anna Holmes. I'm sorry. I've got to go."

Anna scooted back just enough to rise to her feet. The flashlight shown on the corpse and Anna was sure that it was Jolie. The fear within her slowly faded and was replaced with a strange sorrow. Jolie, if that is who she was, just lay there staring up at her. Anna thought of what she had read in the diary. *Jolie had lost her entire family in the war. She and her cousins had come out west with no money, dependent on distant relatives for support. They had paid a price for doing so. Jolie was but eighteen when she became the mistress of the house in Harrison. But if this was her fate, who was buried out by the carriage house?*

Anna slowly turned the flashlight until it was shining on her own face. Then slowly she turned around. “I’ll be back,” Anna said, her voice suddenly calm. She lowered the flashlight slowly and for just a brief moment she saw a woman wrapped in a blanket watching her.

“Good night,” Anna said and turned the light down the passageway and started for the place where the shaft would take her up to the floor above. Anna walked swiftly down the passageway and around the corner. She never looked back until she reached the bottom step of the ladder in the wine cellar. There she paused and shown the light behind her. There was the shadow of a person standing there watching her. The black and red blanket held about her like a robe reminded Anna of the rags she had seen covering the corpse. The figure came closer; the blanket slipped from the head but there was no head. Anna turned and ran up the stairs into the basement. After she closed the trapdoor, Anna pushed the bar back over it. She raced back upstairs to her room and closed the door.

For the next few days Anna was torn between being afraid to stay in the house and afraid to leave Carol there alone. Anna wanted to tell Carol, but it all sounded so childish. “I saw Jolie. She is here in the house. She has been here all the time.”

Carol shared one secret already, the wine cellar. That was enough. Someday Carol would tell Connie about the wine cellar. Telling even that might force the issue. Connie would do something. Anna didn’t know what so she kept quiet. Besides, who would listen if she told them she spoke to a woman who was supposed to have died fifty years ago? Each day Anna tried to tell a different person - her mother - her sister Elizabeth. Each day she stopped herself.

The week before Christmas an alternative presented itself when Anna received a letter from Frank. He told her he was counting the days until he could come back to Idaho. He longed for a white Christmas far away from the mud and rain of the DMZ. He said he would have written more often, but he thought she was away at college and asked what she was doing that winter?

"What am I doing? I'll tell you what I've been up to. It's all your fault. You started it. You made me go down there. Boy! Just wait until you hear what's happened to me."

She wrote him a ten page letter. Then came the hard part, the long wait for a reply.

Every time Anna came to the mansion, she checked to see if the bar had been moved. It was always in the same place over the trapdoor. As long as Connie was home, Carol wasn't likely to try to go down there. Anna wasn't sure if Carol could move the bar by herself. As long as Connie was there, Anna figured the bar would stay right where it was.

For Christmas Anna and her sisters made cookies and her mother baked a pie. In a group the whole family went to the mansion to give them to Carol and Connie. The children ate most of the cookies that night. They sang a few Christmas carols before they left for home.

It was the coldest December Anna could remember but January was colder still. She kept the fire burning when the temperature dropped to twenty-six below a few days later. She read in the paper that the truce was broken and that the B52's were bombing the DMZ again. She hoped that Frank had left the area. It didn't make sense for the Air Force to bomb the area where the army had troops stationed. Perhaps Frank had gotten her letter; perhaps he had been killed in the bombing. She cried and wrote another letter, only five pages this time. She told him of everything that had happened that week from the deep snows and sub-zero temperatures to the Jets winning the AFL Championship.

When the temperature finally rose above zero, the snows began again. The lake was frozen over except for a little pool just west of where the river entered. Snow covering the ice like a white blanket made it look like a valley in winter. One exceptionally cold night the power went out, and Anna stayed downstairs to keep the fire in the fireplace going.

Carol, too, stayed by the fire until late that night. "I wish I could find that blanket Connie brought me. You know the red and black one."

"I'll get you one of the blankets off Connie's bed if you want," Anna replied.

"No, they are all those old heavy ones. I want my new blanket. Come to think of it, I haven't seen it in weeks. You didn't take it up to your room, did you?"

"No, Carol. I don't have your blanket."

That night after Carol finally went to bed, Anna sat near the fire and read in Jolie's diary about a necklace. Jolie described what she called her blue diamonds, the most expensive gift she had ever received.

She wore it only one night for her true love and then hid it in the trunk at the foot of her bed. Anna read through to the end of the diary wondering where Jolie had put the jewels. She thought of asking the woman in the passageway about the necklace but dismissed that. "If you are Jolie, you would know. But if I were Jolie, I wouldn't tell."

The next day Anna asked Carol if she had read the entry about the blue diamonds.

"Oh yes," Carol replied. "At first I thought they might be topaz but Jolie was not a fool about such things."

"And she said blue diamonds?" Anna asked.

"Well, maybe they were sapphires," Carol suggested.

"Would they be valuable?"

"Oh, yes. Even today a sapphire necklace would be very expensive."

"I looked all through the trunk," Anna said.

"Someone else has found them by now. That diary is fifty-years-old. You're almost to the end."

"I read it all. In the last entry she was planning to leave but didn't know just where she would go. She didn't mention packing the necklace. She did describe the fire. Oh my, holy socks! I read it and it didn't even dawn on me. They survived the fire; the last entry in the diary is July 22, 1917. That proves they didn't die in the fire. Jolie isn't buried out there. I bet Dorene and Amiee aren't there either."

Carol nodded; then after a short silence she said, "You think it is a deception?"

"It could be. But why?"

"To see if you are right, we would have to dig up the graves. I wouldn't do that while the ground is frozen." Carol looked over at the fire in the fireplace then added, "Father David asked me not to disturb the graves. And I said I would not."

"But he thinks someone is buried out there. What if instead the neckless is there?"

Carol turned her head slowly toward Anna. For a while she didn't speak but held Anna with her eyes and then she nodded. "You could both be right."

Anna could not take her eyes from Carol's. She had to tell her. "Carol, I know Jolie is not buried out there."

Carol smiled and looked back at the fire. Anna was freed from her eyes.

"Carol, you may not believe me but I saw Jolie. I saw her here in this house."

Carol continued to look into the fire. "Frank said the same thing. He saw someone in the house the night he finished the portrait of Jolie. You two must compare notes or ghost stories."

"I wish Frank were here."

"Frank won't be back until next fall. We've got nothing better to do. Let's look for that necklace."

"Not in the graves," Anna protested.

"How about the rest of the house?"

After they climbed up the stairs to the top floor, Carol sat by the Victrola and looked at the old records while Anna searched the rooms. Slowly they made their way through them searching with the aid of a flashlight for anything related to the women who once lived there. When the power came on that afternoon, Carol suggested they go down to the basement and get a bottle of brandy to warm themselves. Serving the brandy ended the search for the necklace, at least for Carol.

While Carol took a nap by the fireplace, Anna went back downstairs. It was a silly idea but she would ask Jolie if she still had the blue diamond necklace.

Anna had just lifted the trapdoor to the wine cellar when she saw the back wall open. From the shadows just beyond came a voice that, if not for the accent, she might have thought was her own. "So you two have decided to search for my necklace. You can search all you want but you will not find it. When the spring comes I will tell you where to look if you promise to bring it to me. Let me warn you, child; one man has died already when he tried to take that necklace from Jolie. It is mine and always will be mine."

The trapdoor slipped out of Anna hands and dropped shut. She hurriedly pushed the bar over it and ran back upstairs. Then she stopped and for a moment covered her face with her hands. *I can't tell Carol; she will think I'm crazy. She won't hurt me. Jolie hasn't hurt either of us yet. When I find the necklace I will give it to her. That's what she wants.*

That night Anna awoke and sat up quickly in bed. She had dreamed that she was following someone in the catacombs of the house. The figure of a woman with the red and black blanket wrapped tightly around her kept just a short distance ahead of Anna. They traveled without benefit of any light through the bottom level of the passageways all the way to the top floor and into her room. When Anna reached the room, the woman dropped the blanket at the foot of the bed. The lacy black negligee floated across the room until it came to spot where the moonlight shown through the window. Anna stepped closer to see her own image dressed in the black silk. She reached over and turned on the lamp beside the bed and that was when she awoke. "It was so real. Tomorrow will I remember this dream or what I saw in the passageway? Even now I am not sure where the dream began. Oh, I wish Frank were here."

Chapter 13

It was the week before Valentines Day that Anna got a letter from Frank. She took it up to the mansion to read to avoid Elizabeth and her other sisters. Somehow they all knew who the letter was from. Napoleon ran ahead. He was standing on the porch barking when Anna got there. "Won't she let you in today? I don't blame her. You and your big muddy paws. Down! Down! Good Boy!"

The front door was unlocked, the radio was playing loudly, but something was wrong. Anna ran down the hall and into the living room. Carol wasn't there. "Hello! Carol! I'm here."

There was no answer. Anna ran upstairs. No Carol. She quickly ran back down across the living room to the kitchen. Again, no Carol. The door to the basement was open. "Carol? Where are you?"

Anna thundered down the stairs. The bar was pushed aside and the trapdoor was open. "Carol?"

Anna hurried across the room and jumped down into the wine cellar. She landed on one of the boxes and reached down to touch Carol. She was cold. "Carol? Carol?"

Anna felt Carol's neck for a pulse. At the touch of Anna's hand Carol opened her eyes.

"Oh! My God! Carol, I thought you were dead."

"Help me?" Carol's voice trembled as she spoke. "I can't move. I can't move."

"Just lie still. I'll be right back."

"No! Don't leave me again; come back."

Anna raced through the house and down the road. Her father had just arrived home. He never got a chance to get out of his truck. Anna jumped in and told him to drive to the mansion. "Carol fell. She's hurt bad. Hurry!"

"Anna, calm down."

"But we have to hurry."

"Anna! Go have your mother call the sheriff. Go on, get!"

Anna jumped out of the truck. She turned to run for the house and then yelled back at her father. "She's in the basement. Go through the kitchen!"

After calling the fire department, Anna's mother tried to call Judge Parker but had to settle for leaving a message that Carol had fallen and was being taken to Kootenai Medical Center in Coeur d'Alene. Anna begged her mother until she let her go to Coeur d'Alene to be with Carol. On the ride there, Anna listened to the medics radio the hospital that the patient may have a broken hip and was in severe pain.

In the waiting room of the intensive care unit at Kootenai Medical, Anna finally had time to read Frank's letter. He said nothing of what he had been doing the past two months. He did acknowledge her first letter and her adventures in the house in Harrison. He told her that he thought someone had been locked up in the mansion. He had found where they had used the poker from the fireplace to try to get out through the basement door and the chair that had been burned in the fireplace. Frank said he had searched the house for a body but never found one. He speculated that someone could have hidden in the secret passageway when the house was boarded up. After everyone had left, they came out only to find themselves imprisoned in the house. He believed that person was Jolie. Who then, he asked, was buried in her grave. He closed with a suggestion.

"If you want to know what happened to Jolie, ask Father David. I bet he knows just what happened in that house. He would not tell me, but you might be able to charm him. Love, Frank"

"Father David. Hell, I ain't even Catholic," Anna said aloud. "Wait a minute! Love, Frank? What is this? We're just friends, buster! Love, Frank? You've got some nerve."

Anna kissed the letter before she put it away in her purse.

Carol went into surgery that very night. When Anna's father arrived at the hospital, Carol was still in the recovery unit. Anna rode home that night with her father and did not get to see Carol until the following weekend. By then Carol was in her own room and well on the way to recovery. Anna brought some books for Carol who was delighted to get something to read.

"Wonderful! This is so much better than that terrible TV over there. They say I may be here another week. I hope not."

Connie was there that day. She was quiet for most of Anna's visit. When Carol's lunch arrived, Connie suggested that Anna go out with her to get something to eat. They drove to a restaurant just down the road from the medical center. They were seated in a booth which allowed some privacy. Connie kept her voice low as she spoke. "It appears that you and Mother have kept a few secrets from me?"

"Oh! You mean the wine cellar?"

Connie paused, her eyes locked on Anna's. "Yes! You could have been poisoned? You should have known she would try to go down there?"

"It's not my fault."

Connie raised her head looking over Anna not at her. "Why didn't you tell me?"

"So you could take all the liquor out of the house. Her house." Anna spoke through her teeth.

Connie folded her menu. "You're out of order. Answer the question. Why didn't you tell me there was liquor in the house?"

"I didn't tell you because I didn't want you to know. It was our secret. Carol and I are friends. We found the wine cellar. It was our secret."

"Do your parents know?" Connie asked raising her left eyebrow as she spoke.

"They do now. Pa had to help get her out of the cellar. Don't think about suing. He's a volunteer fireman. He knew what he was doing."

Connie's eyes matched the glare in Anna's. "I wasn't thinking that. So your parents know you were drinking? What did they say about that?"

"I had that lecture already."

Connie kept her eyes fixed on Anna. "You also gave an old woman alcohol. What did your parents say about that?"

"We talked about it." Anna's voice began to falter. "She's not that old. I've seen lots of women her age drinking down at the Lakeside Bar. Look, I didn't do anything to hurt Carol. She did it herself. I thought it was safe. I didn't think she could move the bar without my help."

"She's too old to know what is good for her. You knew that."

After taking a deep breath Anna shook her head and then spoke, fighting the urge to yell. "She understands things better than you do. I don't care if you are a judge. Maybe that's your problem. I'm not a criminal; I am Carol's friend. Maybe you don't want her to have any friends?"

"Don't insult me, child."

Anna sat back until her head touched the back of the booth. She felt tears forming in her eyes. "Ma said it was all right. I have no grandmother. She has no granddaughter."

"Your mother said that?"

Anna looked down at the table. "Yes, she did."

"Ha! She did! Well! I don't believe it."

She had won. Anna could not raise her eyes to look across the table. "I don't care if you believe me or not."

Anna waited for the next blow but it didn't come. She looked up. The waiter served coffee. Connie took a sip of the steaming cup. The waiter departed. The stern look slipped slowly away from Connie's eyes. "Mother said almost the same thing. 'She has no grandmother. I have no granddaughter. We shared a little secret. We talked as friends.' I don't know what to do."

Tears started now in Connie's stern eyes. Once started they would not stop. Lunch was over before Connie regained her composure and her sharp critical voice returned. "It's been a trying week. Anna, did Carol tell you any other secrets?"

"What do you mean?"

"You know what I mean. How did you find the wine cellar?"

"It had to be in the basement. We just kept looking until we found it."

"But how did you know it was there?"

"There is a bar in the basement," Anna replied. She looked away; she didn't want to tell Connie about the diary because that would lead to other questions.

"Nothing else?" Connie was now Judge Parker, not her friend.

Anna shrugged her shoulders. "Like what?"

"Well, don't talk to anyone about this. Never mention the house in Harrison to anyone. Do you understand me?"

After lunch they returned to Carol's hospital room. There, with Carol listening, Connie thanked Anna for not only being a friend to Carol but also for acting so quickly when she found Carol had fallen. Then turning to Carol she said, "We gave your little fantasy, a place by the lake, an honest try. It didn't work. I think you should sell the house in Harrison."

"I will not," Carol protested. "I like that old house."

"Now, Mother, don't argue with me. It is in our best interest to sell the house. The sooner the better."

"Connie, try to understand. It wasn't the house. It was the people. It could have happened anywhere."

Connie walked to the door. Nodding her head as if to convey a census, "With a broken leg you can't live in a house like that one. Too many stairs. It also has proven to be too far away from Coeur d'Alene. In the winter that road is treacherous."

"I will not sell. My leg will heal. I will not sell."

"Stop it, Mother. You sound like a parrot."

Anna watched silently. She had never seen the two of them argue so fiercely. Finally Connie shouted, "Keep the house then, but I am not taking you back there. I will never set a foot inside that house again."

"When Frank comes back, I'll have him take me home," Carol shouted in reply.

After Connie stormed out of the room, Anna approached the bed. Carol put out her arms and they shared a long hug.

"She hates me," Carol sobbed.

"She doesn't hate you," Anna whispered back. "She just insists on having her way. She is a judge."

"She was always like that - so damn self-righteous. I told her and now she hates me. I thought I was going to die. Maybe it was the terrible stuff the doctors gave me. It's too late now. Everyone hates me."

Anna held Carol tighter and whispered. "I don't hate you. I love you. We will always be friends."

They held each other a while. Anna felt the tension in Carol's body slowly relax. She kissed her and gently laid her back against the pillows.

Carol closed her eyes, her head pointed up at the ceiling. "Anna, will you adjust this bed. I want to sit up. They don't give you enough pillows in this place."

Anna adjusted the hospital bed into sitting position for Carol. "Now, no more talk about people not liking you. You and Connie just had a fight. Things will be different tomorrow. She is right about one thing."

Carol eased her head back against the pillow. Anna continued. "There are too many stairs in that house for someone with a bum hip. Until it heals, you shouldn't go back there."

Carol wiped her eyes and shook her head. "I tried to tell her, but she got angry, so angry so quickly. She must have guessed what I was going to tell her. She will never understand."

"Carol, I don't know what you're talking about." Anna pulled a chair up beside the bed. "Now, I'm ready to listen. What is this all about?"

"The house in Harrison. He sold it to me. Of course he didn't know who I am. She might tell him. No, she won't do that."

Anna took Carol's hand in hers. "Start from the beginning."

"The beginning? Oh! When did it begin? I guess the war is a good place to start. We lived in France. My father sent me away when the Germans started shelling the city. He and my mother stayed. They said they had to keep the soldiers from looting their shop. We watched from the hill just beyond the farmhouse. The shelling continued all night and the next day the town was gone. Only the church and the bridge were left standing. Jolie's father sent us to the coast. Amiee joined us there. The French were mounting a counter attack; they were going to use Jolie's father's farmhouse as their headquarters."

Anna gripped Carol's hand tighter. Then you must be Dorene.

"We were still in France when we heard that the Germans shelled the farmhouse. Everyone was killed." Carol shut her eyes and her voice became softer. "Jolie had been to England with her father and she spoke the best English so she just took over. I never understood why we moved to this country until I read her diary. At the time I was too afraid to ask questions. While we were in England, we got word that Amiee's family had met the fate same as mine. There was nothing to do but go where Jolie led us. She told the English that she had relatives in America and they let us go on to New York. Jolie had some jewelry, a diamond ring. She sold it in New York to pay for our train tickets to Montana. She also had a way with men to get what we needed. It was not Jolie's fault. She was in shock from losing her family. We were all in shock. It was a way of forgetting. A way of getting what we needed. I told Amiee it would stop when we got to Montana but it didn't. I hated every man I met in Montana, but Jolie told us to smile and laugh. Each time she demanded a higher price for us and still the men would pay it."

Anna leaned over and kissed Carol's hand. "It's all right. You don't have to tell me any more."

"But I do. That is why I bought that house in Harrison. I wanted to show Connie. I wanted to tell her what it was like. It was so different from Montana. It was all those Marshall boys. Those handsome men with their wide smiles and big hands. We met them on the train. We had planned to go on to Seattle but they got off in Spokane and persuaded us to do so too. We knew they had left their wives behind in Montana. It was just for the weekend."

Anna saw the tears forming in Carol's pale blue eyes. "Carol. I would have done the same thing."

"Then it turned out to be true. It was even in the newspaper."

"You lost me," Anna said.

"The story they told us. We didn't believe it for a minute." Carol looked directly at Anna. "They said they had come to Spokane for a funeral. Their sister-in-law had died. Jolie laughed when they asked if she would cheer up their brother Bradley in his time of loss. But it was true. And the moment Jolie saw James Bradley Marshall IV she agreed. Did she ever cheer him up? Amiee and I had to bring food to her room at the hotel for three days. Finally Bradley left. We were going to get back on the train the next day, but the hotel tossed us out that night. Jolie took a carriage to Bradley Marshall's house. It was a fine house on the south hill overlooking Spokane. His two brothers from Montana were staying there. I never went inside but Jolie did."

Anna held Carol's hand tight, wishing she would stop talking but she seemed to grow stronger.

Carol nodded her head. "That very night we traveled by electric train and steamboat to the house in Harrison. It was so different. It was like a dream. In the house we were called by our name, treated with respect. We were even given monthly allowances for food and clothing. But we did not deceive ourselves. We were there for their pleasure. Jolie told us we would spend the winter in Harrison and move in the summer. We planned to leave. We did. I tell you. I wanted to tell Connie. We planned to leave. We put some of the money aside each month. It's no use. God may forgive me but my own family never will."

"Frank will and someday Connie will too," Anna promised her.

"Oh! I could never tell Frank. A man would never understand."

"I'll tell him," Anna countered. "And if he doesn't understand, he's history."

"But would he understand murder?"

"Tell me what happened," Anna whispered.

Carol closed her eyes and then opened them slowly. She looked past Anna at the door. Anna turned to see Judge Parker standing there. "It's late. Mother needs her rest. You must leave now."

Carol was in the hospital for a week. She spent the next month in a nursing home. Connie came back to Harrison only once. She got a few things from the house and left the key with Anna.

"I am trying to persuade my mother to sell the place. It just won't work. I need to be in Coeur d'Alene and now the stairs will be too much for her. She asked me to give you the key to the house. Keep the heat on and look after the place for her. I don't want any damage. It will bring a good price someday."

"Can I still go there?" Anna asked.

"Of course you can. Stay out of the wine cellar. Oh! One more thing! Father David is back in Spokane. He's staying at the Jesuit House at Gonzaga. Last Sunday he got a ride over and stopped in to see Mother. His problem right now is transportation. He can't drive anymore. Mother suggested when the weather is better you should take him the book. I guess you know what she is talking about." Carol looked at Anna as if she expected her to pull the book out of her pocket.

"Oh! I think I know what book she is talking about. It's just an old book," Anna said. "It's - it's in French."

Carol shook her head and said, "Would you see that he gets it? Mother seems to think it is important."

Chapter 14

Once more Jolie found the house deserted. No one came there for almost a week. She walked through the room on the third floor each night. Anna had left some clothes there, which meant she planned to return. "She must return. I cannot stand this silence."

Jolie stood at the window and looked out at the rain. It was rain that changed the season from winter to spring. "Anna will return. She is too curious to stay away. Someday that boy, Frank, will return. A man will always return to his first love. And what of my first true love? Maybe this will be the spring that he will remember and return to find me. No, it has been too long. I must not hope."

Anna pushed Carol in her wheelchair down the hall of the hospital. "Tomorrow you will be going home. You should be cheerful."

"I won't be going back to my house in Harrison. I will be going to a nursing home here in Coeur d'Alene. Why should I be happy about that?"

Anna pulled the wheelchair quickly to the side of the hall to allow two nurses to wheel a gurney down the hall. After they passed, Anna continued her circle of the third floor of the hospital. "Carol, you can't go back to the house in Harrison until you can walk."

"I wish Frank were back. He'd help me get back to Harrison. He liked that old house."

As they approached Carol's hospital room, a slightly built man in a perfectly tailored dark blue suit walked briskly past. Carol turned her head sharply and watched him as he went down the hall.

"Do you know him?" Anna asked.

Carol shook her head. "I am not sure. I have only seen his picture in the paper. But what would he be doing here?"

Ann wheeled Carol to her bedside. "Okay, you have me curious. Who was that handsome rich dude?"

Carol smiled. "If I am correct, he is Bradley Marshall the Fifth. The son of the man who built the house in Harrison."

"But you said that Father David owned that house."

"Yes, Brad Marshall is Father David's half-brother. He looks remarkably like his father."

A few minutes later Anna walked silently down the hallway. The man in the dark blue suit was standing in the hallway just beyond the next doorway on the left side of the hall. Anna could hear the voice of an older man almost yelling in the room. She slowed her pace and looked in as she walked past the room.

"They were big men. Two of them. I don't know why they attacked me. I never saw them before."

"What did they look like?"

"Twins. Two huge twin monsters. I bet they each weighed three-hundred pounds."

As Anna continued past the room, the man in the dark blue suit didn't even look her way. She smiled. *So that's what the man who built the house in Harrison looked like? Did your father eavesdrop at hospital room doors too? I think I will have a talk with your brother. Maybe he can tell me more about you and your father.*

Each morning Jolie watched from the window. On the fifth day of her vigil that week, Jolie saw a long black car pull into the driveway. It stopped just past the carriage house. The driver quickly got out of the car and went to the passenger door and opened it. A man much shorter than the driver stepped out into the rain. Jolie stepped back from the window. "Who is this? Another thief?"

The short man in the long grey raincoat walked slowly to the three graves. Jolie gasped and her hand came to her lips as she watched the man kneel as if in prayer. "It is him. After all these years he has returned."

She raised the silver dagger and touched the point. "How should I greet him? Is he the man who left me imprisoned in this house or the one who comes to rescue me?"

But the visitors did not come to the house. They departed shortly, leaving behind three baskets of flowers.

Jolie spent that entire day in the room on the third floor. She lay in the bed and rested. She looked through the books that Anna had left behind. Often she returned to the window to view the flowers on the graves across the yard. It was late in the afternoon when she saw another car enter the driveway. This one did not stop at the carriage house but came directly to the mansion. When Jolie heard the front door open, she hurried back to the closet and from there to the safety of the passageways.

He was in the dining room when she finally made her way through the narrow passageways to the first floor. From the hidden chamber beside the fireplace she spied on him. The flash from his camera blinded her. She stood there behind the wall and tracked his movement by sound alone until she could see again. He was a heavy-set man with a bald head. He photographed all the paintings on the wall. Then he proceeded swiftly through the house one room at a time. Jolie could not move fast enough to track him. By the time she reached the second floor he had moved to the third. Jolie descended through the passageways to the basement and waited for him there.

Heavy footsteps shook the stairs to the basement. Jolie closed the closet door and waited. There were but three flashes through the crack in the doorframe and she heard his footsteps going back up the stairs.

Jolie opened the closet door and followed him up the stairs. When she reached the kitchen she heard the front door being closed. From the living room she watched as he backed his car around and drove back down the driveway.

At the carriage house he stopped. Through the rain Jolie could still see the flash as he took a picture of each of the graves before departing.

Jolie checked the front door. It was locked. "This man had a key. He will return. I need help. I cannot alone defend this house from strangers. If only Frank or Anna would return."

It was a Sunday afternoon, the only sunny Sunday Anna remembered in several weeks. Father David arranged for her to eat lunch at the Jesuit House. It seemed strange to Anna to be eating with four men, all of whom she assumed were elderly priests.

After the meal Father David suggested they take a walk across the Gonzaga campus and enjoy the pleasant weather. While he went upstairs to get his jacket Anna waited in the hall. She looked at the four oil paintings in the hallway while she waited. All were churches, very old churches. One she recognized as Notre Dame from the movie she had seen. It was signed simply with the initials D. M.

"Rain is needed but it is such a joy when the sun reappears after a long absence," Father David said. "Now, what is it you wanted to talk to me about?"

"The house in Harrison," Anna replied.

"My father had the house built for the family but it also served his business as well. Mother and I would spend the summers there. In the winter after we moved back to Spokane, Father would take business associates, those interested in investing in the mining or lumber industry, there. It was a logical stopping point on the way back from Kellogg and it was the center for the lumber industry."

"Who are the three women buried there?"

"I would rather not go into that," Father David said bluntly.

"Come now, Father; certainly you would have met them if you spent the summers there?"

Father David glanced her way but continued his slow but steady pace.

"Are you an artist?" Anna asked.

He frowned but nodded in reply.

"I saw the paintings of the churches back there. Did you do them?"

"Oh, those. Yes, I have painted sixteen of the oldest churches in western Europe," he replied with a laugh.

Anna smiled. She waited a few seconds before she asked. "Did you do the portraits of Amiee, Dorene and Jolie?"

"Yes," he acknowledged. "It was after Mother died. One day in late July I packed up my art supplies and went to stay at the house in Harrison. I was shocked at what I found. They wouldn't let me in my house. I stayed at the hotel down on the waterfront and returned to Spokane the next day. Father thought it was all very funny."

Anna watched his eyes as she asked. "You did return. You had to. You did the portraits. They were done in that house."

She was sure he was trying not to smile. His cheeks were just a little pink. "Yes, I returned several times that summer to the house in Harrison."

Anna stopped and searched in her purse until she found the book and handed it to him without a word.

He looked at it for a minute and then opened it to the first page. "Did you find this in the house?"

"Yes. It's Jolie's -"

"It's her diary. It is not mine." He held it out for Anna to take but she shook her head.

"Carol Potter wanted you to read it. She said it was important. You would understand after you read the diary."

"No, I don't think I should." He protested.

Anna noticed the book shake in his hand. "She didn't die in the fire," she whispered. "Please read the book. Carol wants you to understand."

His eyes were wide. "She didn't die in the fire?"

They walked without speaking a word until they came to the hill overlooking the baseball field. "If Jolie did not die in the fire, what of the others?"

"There are three graves. But Jolie and Dorene are not buried there," Anna replied. "Frank said to ask you what happened in Harrison. He thought you might know."

"How do you know that Dorene and Jolie are not buried in those graves?"

"I cannot tell you how I know."

"And I cannot tell you what happened in Harrison."

"Am I only to believe what is written in Jolie's diary and what Carol has told me?"

His hands stopped shaking. He put the small black book in his coat pocket. "Jolie's diary and what Carol has told me" - he repeated her sentence then added, "Carol! The house was never put on the market. She just wrote to me and offered to buy it. I had many problems at the time so I didn't think much about it. Now you imply that she knew of the house and what happened there. There is only one way she would know. She is Dorene, is she not?"

"Yes, Father." Anna shook her head. *Damn! Now I have no more information to trade. I had hoped you would say more before I told you that Carol is Dorene. I won't tell you about the secret passageways unless you tell me about Jolie and the blue-diamond necklace.*

He turned and started back across campus at a slow pace. "Walking is good for my heart, the doctors say. There has been so much rain I haven't been out much. I knew the affair with the house in Harrison would not last. That it lasted even a year is surprising. My uncles had already grown tired of the charade. They were making monthly trips back to see their families in Montana. Father held on to the end, even after he was engaged to be married again. The fire didn't really end it. He had already sent Uncle Ethan to Harrison to send the women packing. After the fire my father and I went to Harrison. It was the strangest experience of my life."

As they walked, he talked in a low voice and Anna struggled to hear him.

"I can remember those days as if they happened yesterday. When word of the fire at Harrison reached my father, he telephoned my uncles in Spokane and ordered them to check on the house in Harrison before returning to Montana. He and his bride took the train east from Seattle that very night. You see, they were on their honeymoon when the fire occurred. I met them at the train station. I was a young lad and news of the fire had me very upset, so I insisted on going to Harrison with him.

After settling his bride in our home here in Spokane, we took the electric train to Coeur d'Alene and from there a steamer down the lake to Harrison. God forgive me, but I never liked the woman. She was not at all like Mother.

It had been four days since the fire started when we stopped on the dusty road to look down at the town of Harrison. I remember it was a hot day and I had to wipe the sweat from my brow, lest it get in my eyes. I could see the fire was still burning. In fact, it looked like four different fires.

"They'd better put them out before they get some wind," Father said, "or they risk losing the rest of the town."

I told him that I had read in the Coeur d'Alene paper that they were going to rebuild. Harrison would be better than it was before the fire.

"Not likely," he countered and continued up the hill.

I argued that the governor said the state would give them $5,000 to start to rebuild. Father never walked anywhere; he marched. I used to try to match his stride for I was almost as tall as he, but I never could.

"Political talk, that's all it is," Father said. "Moses will promise them anything just to keep his job as governor."

"But he gave the mayor a check," I argued.

"So far the state has only given Harrison $1,000. That won't get the job done," he declared.

"But they will rebuild? They must."

"Watch the boats. More people are leaving every day. Now the fate of Harrison depends on the lumber companies. If they rebuild, fine. If not, forget Harrison. The railroads link directly to Kellogg and Wallace, so mining can bypass Harrison. The Wobbles may have won." Father stopped to look at the deacon's house as we passed.

"Do you think that the I. W. W. was behind the fire?" I asked.

"Of course, they were. With us joining the war they will be even more active. Look at the Russians; they are just giving the battlefield to the Huns."

We turned back up the hill and looked up at the mansion half hidden by the young trees growing around it. This was the largest and grandest house in Harrison. Now it stood boarded up; not a single window showed.

"Hey, Davie, look at that!" Father said, pointing up at the house. "They even boarded up the third-floor windows. That's Samuel for you. Either a job is half done or overdone."

"Where did they go?" I asked.

"Where did your Uncle Ethan go? That's the question. According to Samuel, the girls never left."

"What?" I couldn't believe it.

"Come over here," he said.

Father led me across the grass to the carriage house. There in the shadows of the pine trees were three fresh graves. I remember kneeling to read the grave markers and then saying a prayer. "Did they die in the fire?"

"No, I don't think so," Father replied. "No one else died in the fire. Half the town burned down and these were the only three that died. Ha! I'll never believe that. Look around. The fire never even got this far."

"Then what happened?" I was still kneeling beside the graves.

"I sent Ethan to close down the place and send the girls away. My guess is he screwed it up. That Jolie is a wildcat; she probably put up a fight. If he killed her, he would have had to kill the other two. Then the dummy buried them here and ran. The fire may have worked to his advantage. So far no one is investigating their death."

"Uncle Ethan killed them?"

I couldn't believe it. Keeping three women there in Harrison was bad enough. They couldn't have killed them. Father wasn't very reassuring. He said. "Now I don't know that for sure. I sent him here to root them out. It's the deacon down there who said they died in the fire and he buried them on my property."

"Why don't you believe him?" I asked.

"Where's Ethan? See it don't fit. Now if Ethan killed them and then bribed the deacon to back up his story that the girls died in the fire, that fits."

"Bribed a deacon?" Father was always critical of the clergy of all faiths.

"Sure the clergy are the easiest people to bribe. That's how they make their living, taking money from people who feel guilty about something."

"Mother wouldn't agree with you," I said as I rose to my feet.

"Your mother is dead. I have a new wife now. I don't want to hear any of this stepmother bull from you. You will address her as Mother and with respect."

"I have always addressed both of you with respect, but she is not my mother," I told him. I so wanted to assert myself back then. "I'm sixteen; I can't call a woman who is only two years older than I am, mother."

"In my house you will do just that," he declared.

That is when I told him. I stood up as tall as I could and looked him directly in the eye. "I will go away. With a new bride, you don't want me around. I don't believe she does either."

"If you're thinking of joining the army, forget it. The damn war will be over soon. It's not our war anyway."

I calmly folded my arms across my chest and stared back at him. It was time for me to leave home and he knew it.

"Look at yourself, David. You're not fit for war. You're too soft. Hell, you're still a boy."

"I wasn't talking about joining the army. I plan to enter the seminary."

"No, I won't allow it. You need to grow up first. Too bad the girls are gone. A night with them and you'd forget all about the priest nonsense."

"I have completed all my studies for high school," I declared. "The Jesuits have a seminary just north of Spokane. I won't be far away. Mother wanted me to be a priest, and I want to give it a try. Maybe it's the best life for me."

"One night in here would have changed your mind," Father laughed as he said it. "There are others. Not like these three but still good enough for a youngster like you. I'll arrange it."

"Father, I have made up my mind. Why try to dissuade me? Think of your bride. Do you really want another man in the house whose just learning about women?" Perhaps now I think I shouldn't have said that but I was young then. His reply was sharp.

"Watch you tongue. I'll belt you from here to the house."

"Well, at least you got my point." I turned and looked toward the mansion. "I'm going to the seminary. It may not work out, but I will give it my best. Now is the time to do that - best for me and best for you."

In reply Father walked past me toward the house. I followed in silence. At the steps to the porch he stopped.

"I'm going to wait," he said. "I want to see what the lumber companies do before I decide if I'll sell this house. It may be a lost investment."

"The house is a lost investment? What of the women? What of your brother, Ethan? You're callous."

"You're soft. Maybe the seminary is a good place for you. At least you will be safe if there is a draft." He folded his arms across his chest. "The women earned their keep. You don't understand. You're not a man yet. We needed them. They got paid for it. As for Ethan, he always was a misfit. Samuel told me that Ethan took all the money we had here. Bet he took all the money the girls had too. He'll hobble around in style for a while and then come limping home. A priest in the family! Ha! Maybe we need one. We are a wild lot."

It was the closest my father ever came to approving of my vocation. Even then he held out an alternative.

"Tell you what I'll do for you, Mister David Marshall. I will give you the House in Harrison. It's yours. I'll even help you hire some girls if that's what you want. But you must never mention it to my new wife. If someday you want to quit your church job, you have a place to live."

I didn't go inside the house that day for we had no lanterns and the place was boarded up.

They walked along in silence for a while; then he spoke again. "When Mrs. Potter offered to buy the house, I was relieved. It was a burden I didn't have to carry anymore. Still, at the time I was reluctant to do so. If I was not going to have heart surgery the next day I probably would not have sold it."

Father David stopped and looked at Anna. “If Jolie is not buried in that grave, where is she?”

Anna smiled. “If you come to Harrison, I will show you.”

Chapter 15

When Anna returned from Spokane, she cleaned all the rooms on the first floor of the mansion. Father David had promised to come to Harrison, but he had not said when he would come. She wanted the house to look presentable if he did. She told her mother and Elizabeth that she would be staying at the mansion. Her mother argued against Anna staying alone in that big house but Elizabeth welcomed the news for she now had a bed of her own. They reached a compromise and Anna agreed to eat all her meals at home. She soon learned to like the arrangement for the house did seem empty and lonely without Carol. At night Anna would leave the light on in her bedroom and sometimes she would forget and leave it on when she left.

Saturday night, Jolie entered the room after Anna had fallen asleep. She waited for her eyes to adjust to the light.

"Foolish child, why do you sleep with the light on? Darkness is a friend not a foe. I saw you pretending to clean the house and all the while looking for my necklace. Now somehow I must recruit you to my side. You must help me or we will both lose the necklace to those strangers."

For a long time Jolie just stood at the foot of the bed where Anna slept. Like slowly moving waves, feelings of anger, envy, pity and love moved through her.

"I hate you, for you are alive and living in my room in my house. I cry for you, for you have lost your love, like I lost mine. Men - they just go away. Most of all I need you. When this house is empty, I am nothing. I will comfort you, but you must do something for me. You must dig up the grave. You must bring me my necklace."

Jolie approached the side of the bed. She leaned over and whispered softly, "Anna. Anna, listen to me. The necklace is here. Forget what the old woman said. Look out the window. When the sunlight strikes my grave. Look. Look. Where would you hide something so valuable? My necklace, it is so beautiful. Find it. Find it before that old woman returns."

On the table beside the bed was a letter. Jolie picked it up, read it and then returned it to the table. "This boy, Frank - he will return. She needs him and so do I. He would willingly dig up a grave. He is the answer to both our prayers."

She reached out and touched Anna's hand. The girl jumped like she had a chill but she didn't awake. Jolie turned from the bed at the sound of an old truck in the driveway. She stepped to the windows and saw the headlights pass the carriage house. Jolie raised her hand to her face. "They come by night. This will be trouble."

Anna reached for the covers only to find they had been pulled back. She sat up in bed and looked around. At the sound of a car engine she jumped out of bed and moved to the window. *Now who could that be?*

"Hide. To the closet. Quickly, child."

Anna turned at the voice behind her. She could see no one in the room, but the closet door was open wide. Anna moved quickly to the closet. The door closed behind her. She heard the double click of the closet door and stepped back for she knew the trapdoor in the floor would open just where she was standing. "I have no light. I will be lost."

"Trust me, Anna. I will lead you. Move quickly; they have entered the house."

Anna slipped into the passageway and carefully down the ladder. When she closed the trapdoor above her, Anna felt another hand in hers. "Come, child; we must see what they are doing."

Relying on her memory of the narrow shafts and tunnels, Anna followed where the soft hand led her. When they reached the main floor, Anna could hear voices through the walls.

"I want another photograph of that painting."

There was a flash of light through the pinholes in the wall just to Anna's right. She turned sideways in the narrow passageway. *Ah! Now I know where we are. This is the chamber beside the fireplace. And that was the flash of a camera. So they are photographing Jolie's painting. I bet I know why.*

A deeper voice replied. "How about the other paintings?"

"No. Just that one."

"So we are looking for the jewels?"

"I didn't say that."

"Hell! The girl has been dead for years. We ain't here for her. If it ain't the jewels, what are we looking for?"

Anna felt Jolie push her aside. She moved to her right until her left eye could see through the pinhole on the right. She felt Jolie brush against her and knew that she was watching though the other pinhole.

"My God!" Jolie gasped. "It is Brad Marshall. It can't be. He should be dead by now."

Anna turned her head and whispered. "That is his son. He is Father David's half-brother."

Anna felt a hand grip her arm. "Father David! David became a priest. How dare he?"

Anna moved her head a little, searching the room as best she could through the small hole in the wall. The two men were no longer there.

"This way," Jolie whispered. "They have gone to the kitchen. I bet they are headed for the basement."

Anna followed Jolie back through the tunnel under the living room and down the ladder on the rounded pillar to the basement level. There was no exit from the passageways on the main floor of the house so Jolie slowly made her way to the next lower level. But when they entered the closet and looked out through the door, they saw only the dark room.

Anna reached out and felt for Jolie beside her. "The light! I left the light on in my room. They must have gone up to check."

"Do not fear, Anna. We are safe in here."

"But they will know that I am living here."

"Wait and listen. By the time we could reach my room they will have started back down."

Anna felt her legs begin to shake; then she felt Jolie's arm around her. Instinctively, as if it were her sister Elizabeth, Anna hugged the woman beside her. *I can't believe that I am hugging a ghost.*

Then her left hand slipped smoothly over the silky robe until it touched something solid. Lightly her fingers traced the outline of a dagger tucked in the pocket of the robe. Anna's hand froze. Just then she heard voices coming down the steps to the basement.

"Don't talk so loud."

"Hell, Mr. Marshall, believe me; there is no one here."

"Someone turned on that light."

"I tell you it's just a trick. They leave a light on in the house so a burglar will think someone is home. Both the old ladies are in Coeur d'Alene. I checked."

"The things in that bedroom don't belong to an old lady."

"So what, the bitch ain't here. If she was, it would be more interesting."

The lights in the basement room flashed on. Anna pulled the door closed and stepped to the back panel of the closet.

"Turn off those lights!"

"Relax, Mr. Marshall! You're going to have a heart attack. No windows down here, so why flounder around in the dark?"

Anna had just squeezed past the back panel of the closet when she heard the closet doorknob click as it turned. *What if he knows about the passageway?*

Anna tried to retreat down the passageway but she felt Jolie block her way. A thin beam of light entered the darkness and reflected off the cold steel of a dagger.

"You looking for ghosts in the closet?"

"Never mind what I am looking for."

"Hey, how can I find something if I don't know what I'm looking for?"

The closet door closed. Anna breathed a deep sigh. Her head rolled back on her shoulders. *Don't faint now. I can't make any noise. I must not faint.*

Anna felt Jolie's arms around her. "Be brave. You are safe here."

Anna tried to tell where in the room the two men were from the sound of their voices.

"A bar and no liquor! What a waste!"

"I bet there is a wine cellar under the bar."

Jolie whispered, "Anna, open the panel to the closet."

Anna felt in the darkness until she found the handle to the entrance to the closet. She closed her eyes, turned the handle and stepped forward. A thin ray of light marked the top of the door leading to the main room in the basement. “Now open the door just a crack.”

Anna bit her tongue as her fingers touched the door handle. She pushed the door just a hair forward. She felt Jolie brush forward to peek into the room. Anna stooped down and leaned forward to look through the crack into the room.

“Hey! How did you know that?”

“My uncle built this house. He also built the one I’m living in. He had his tricks.”

Anna could see both of the two men now. The second man was much larger than Brad Marshall. He was looking down at the stairs that led to the wine cellar. *If you know about the wine cellar, do you know about the entry to these passageways?*

“He going down,” Anna whispered.

“He’s after liquor. He is not important,” Jolie replied. “Watch what the son does once his lackey is down the stairs.”

Anna pressed her face against the door. She saw Brad step quickly to the fireplace. He tried to shift the stones along the left corner of the fireplace. He started at the top and proceeded down to the bottom. Then he hurriedly tried the other side of the fireplace. The third stone he tried rotated to the left and he stooped to look inside.

Anna heard Jolie whisper, “Sorry Monsieur Brad, but you are years too late. We took the money from that hiding place long ago.”

The second man came up the stairs from the wine cellar carrying two bottles.

“Don’t drink that,” Brad called from across the room.

“Why not?”

“It’s been down there for over fifty years; it is probably vinegar by now. Anyway, we’re through here. Come on! Let’s go. I want to look upstairs.”

“Brandy? Brandy don’t turn to vinegar.”

The man protested until Brad told him he could take the bottle with him.

Anna felt Jolie pull on her arm so she turned and followed this shadow of a woman back into the passageways. She found she could travel faster if she closed her eyes. But when she did she also saw the ghost of Jolie beside her. *Frank was right; you do look like me. But you must have died fifty years ago. What are you leading me into?*

When they reached the chamber beside the fireplace, both men were in the living room.

"Do you have a shovel in the truck?"

"Maybe."

"You don't know."

"Hell, I stole it just a half-hour before I picked you up. You didn't say anything about needing a shovel."

"Go look."

Anna watched and as soon as the other man had left the room Brad went to the fireplace. Like the ones downstairs the stones were large but closely-fitted. He tried each stone on the corners and failed to find any hiding place there. He turned his flashlight on the portrait of Jolie and walked over to view it closely just as the second man returned to the room.

"No shovels. What were you going to dig up anyway?"

"The graves," Brad answered. "Remember to bring shovels next time. Bring a pick too; that dirt will be well settled after fifty years. How long will it take to dig up a grave?"

"Hell, I don't know. Maybe two hours."

Brad snapped off his flashlight. "How long if you got the Kato brothers to help?"

"They don't do stuff like that. You got someone else you want hurt bad, they do that."

The voices were fading fast. Anna held her breath and pressed her ear against the pinhole in the wall.

"What if I wanted someone killed?"

Anna never heard the answer to that last question. In silence she followed Jolie back through the passageways to her room. It was not until she entered the lighted bedroom that she began to shake.

She sat on the side of the bed. *Was this all a bad dream? I can't stay here but if I leave what will happen? Jolie is no match for these two. They will dig up the graves. They must be looking for the blue-diamond necklace. I can't let them get it. And who does Brad Marshall want killed? Could it be Carol?*

Chapter 16

Anna walked up the soggy road to the house in Harrison with Napoleon following. At the porch she wiped the mud off her shoes before unlocking the door and going inside. Trips to Coeur d'Alene to see Carol, her work schedule and the rain had all conspired to limit her visits to the old house. "Stay here, Napoleon. You're too dirty to come inside. I'm not scared to be alone in here."

The big dog stuck his nose in the doorway as soon as Anna opened it. "No. Stay on the porch."

Anna went straight to the stairs and started up them without turning on any lights. She could just as well have stopped and read the letter in the living room but she didn't. At the third floor she found the door to her bedroom closed.

"The wind. Oh, yes. The wind blows the door shut but only if the window is open," Anna said aloud. She walked into the room and nodded at the open window. "Someday I will have to get a doorstop."

There was no reply but Anna looked in the closet to see if Jolie was there. She walked back to the bed and turned around slowly. The bed was a mess but she had left it that way. The lamp on the little table beside it was on, but Anna knew that she often forgot and left it on herself. "I know you were here. You're watching me aren't you? Well, I don't care. At home I have five pairs of eyes watching me all the time."

Anna fluffed up the pillows and sat down. Carefully she opened the letter. Instead of beginning with Frank's usual comments on the weather it began with these words, "I hate war."

In an almost state of shock, Anna read Frank's tale. His squad was ambushed just as they approached a small village in the mountains. Pinned down by sniper fire they called for air support. Three Heughies arrived quickly and strafed the village.

When we entered the village, we found six dead Vietcong. At least six of the bodies had weapons beside them. We buried them and the bodies of thirty other including ten children.

Anna's tears fell on the letter as she read. "Just come home,

Frank. Just come home alive."

The rain was not coming inside but the cold night air was. Anna rose from bed to close the window. She turned off the night light beside the bed and looked out into the yard. "Frank, I wish you were here. Of course it might be a little embarrassing; I was sleeping in your bed. Nothing we couldn't work out. An arrangement of convenience, that's what the Marshall brothers had."

Anna sat back on the bed. It was then that she noticed the figure in the blanket standing in the closet doorway.

"Come in," Anna said. "After all, this was your room."

The shadowy figure advanced slowly. Anna peered at the blanket where it shaded the face.

The voice sounded like a low wind. "They will return tonight. They will come to dig up the graves. We must stop them."

Anna could feel her legs begin to shake on the bed. In the dark she could not see but a shadow where Jolie's face should be. Anna closed her eyes and then she saw a face as beautiful as the one in the portrait that hung on the wall downstairs. *This strange woman, she bewitched Frank. He painted the necklace into her portrait and now she beckons me to help her find that necklace. Oh Frank! I wish you were here.*

The shadowy figure advanced into the soft light in the window. The blanket dropped to the figure's shoulders as she extended her right hand. Anna instinctively raised her right hand to her lips. The hair and the face were but a shadow in the dark. For just a moment Anna closed her eyes and she beheld the beautiful Jolie just as Frank had painted her in the portrait. "I have talked with Father David. He told me of this house and how he painted the first set of portraits. Was he one of your lover?"

"A woman only has one true lover. We will talk of that later. Tonight there is danger in the air."

"How many did you kill with that dagger you carry? Frank described it as a silver dagger and somehow even in the dark I can see it is so."

"I need your help."

"You need me." Anna laughed. The shadow near the window turned and looked her way. Anna felt a shiver from her head to her toes. She nodded. "I will help you. You led me back here when I was lost in the darkness. I will help you."

"Come closer. Stand by the window in the light of the moon."

Anna slid her legs off the bed and stepped to the window.

"Do not fear me. There are others who will comes. You must be brave, child."

Anna closed her eyes at the sound of Jolie's voice and felt her hand on her shoulder, but she did not look her way. "Fear you? All you care about is your damn necklace and I don't have it."

"The necklace was a precious gift and now it will be the cause of evil. Be brave, Anna. Together we can keep them for finding my necklace. I can feel it in my bones. They will come back tonight."

"Not on a night like tonight," Anna replied.

"They will come tonight. After the rain stops and the moon appears they will come to dig up the graves. We must kill them."

Anna felt her legs wobble. She reached out to the wall to keep her balance. "I will not kill for you but I will help you keep your necklace. Tell me first what happened here in the house so long ago."

"This house and I must keep our secrets."

"I have learned much already. I know that Dorene did not die in the fire."

"How would you know that?"

Anna heard her own voice had dropped to a whisper and she tried to speak louder. "Dorene was here. She returned to the house and you did not even recognize her. The old woman, Mrs. Potter is Dorene. She slept in the room on the second floor. She also found your diary and gave it to me to read."

"Dorene? My own cousin? I knew there was something familiar about her. And she put you up to this, to steal my necklace."

For a moment Anna wondered if the silver dagger would suddenly appear again from beneath the blanket. She stepped back. She felt the wall against her hips. Anna swallowed hard and looked up over the shadowy figure.

"Yes, we looked for the necklace. But that is not why she bought this house. Mrs. Carol Potter was trying to tell her family what happened here in Harrison."

Jolie turned and looked out the window off toward the carriage house. "Some things are best left alone."

"Frank is Dorene's grandson. Someday she wants to explain to him about this house in Harrison."

The figure bowed her head. "He is a man. He will never understand."

Anna stepped closer to the presence at the window. "When he returns, Dorene will tell him everything and so will I."

"No. It must remain a secret."

Anna put her hand to her lips. "If you were not a ghost, I would swear that you were crying."

The figure raised the blanket to her face. Anna reached out until she held the blanket in both hands. She pulled until Jolie raised her head and look her way. "If neither you nor Dorene are buried out there who is?"

"Your question will soon be answered. We will let them dig up the graves before we kill them. I have a dagger; you should get a knife from the kitchen. There will be two of them; the big one is yours. I hope they do not bring others to help them."

Anna stepped between the shadow of Jolie and the window. "I will not kill for you."

Jolie stepped back.

Anna advanced. "Is this precious necklace of yours buried in one of the graves?"

Jolie did not answer.

Anna nodded. "So that is it. The necklace is buried in one of the graves. It is beginning to make sense. Father David told me that he thought you had all died in the fire so he never went into the house. Frank wrote me that he thought someone was trapped here in the house when it was boarded up. You were the one trapped here. Dorene escaped. Did Amiee escape too?"

Anna felt Jolie's hand on hers. "They left together, the morning before the Marshall brothers arrived. Enough of this talk we must get ready for tonight."

Anna shook her head. "We can't kill two men and bury them before dawn. We must think of something else to do. Maybe they will not come tonight."

Anna turned and walked back to the window.

Silently Jolie came to her. "You are right; it cannot be done so quickly. We must lure them to this house. If we can trick them into entering the wine cellar, we can kill them there."

Anna reached over and turned on the lamp beside the bed. She turned toward Jolie but saw only a shadow where her face and hair should be. "We wait. I do not think that Brad Marshall will return on such a rainy night but he will come again to the house. I know he will. Now tell me what happened in this house that summer fifty years ago."

The ghostly figure turned away from the light but she did not leave.

"There were four Marshall brothers. Brad was the leader, for he was the oldest. Ethan, they didn't even treat like a brother. He was the man who built this house."

Anna felt her heart race; she could not let this chance go by but suddenly she feared she would learn something she didn't want to know. For a moment she remembered her last visit with Carol in the hospital and Anna reached out and put her hand over Jolie's hand. "God would forgive you. Tell me what happened. I will understand. I will forgive you too. Give me a chance. What happened here?"

There was a hint of laughter in Jolie's reply, "Forgive yes, but do not try to understand."

"I promise."

Chapter 17

That night after Jolie had left, Anna pulled the covers up tight to her chin. “Oh I wish Frank were here. I need him.”

In her dreams he was there. She was posing for him in the basement beside the fireplace. Her dream followed the events of the night faithfully until she kissed him; then she felt herself rise into the air. She spun. She fell. She rose again. He held her so close that she could not breathe. Togther they spun wildly, tumbling as they fell. With a shriek they flew skyward.

The light was too bright. Anna sat up quickly in bed. The air was cold, her blanket tossed to the side of the bed.

“You had a dream.”

Anna searched the room for Jolie. There just to the left of the window was a form of a young woman in a black silk gown.

“They are here.”

Anna rubbed her eyes and walked to the window. Out beside the carriage house was a pickup truck. It was turned so that the headlights were directed to the three graves. From the tail lights Anna could tell it was a big old four-wheel drive rig.

“It is that Brad Marshall and that man who came with him before.”

Anna stepped back from the window and quickly pulled on her jeans and sweater. “Are they coming to the house?”

“No, they have a lantern and shovels. You will have to lure them here.”

Anna knelt down to put on her shoes. “A man who wears a three-piece suit does not dig graves. Brad Marshall will come to the house.”

“They must both come or our plan will fail. Where is your knife?”

Anna jumped to her feet and started for the door. She glanced out the window just before she left the room. She saw only one man digging at the site of the first grave. *I knew Brad Marshall would not dig.*

Anna hurried down the first flight of stairs. She had just gone past

Carol's room on the second floor when she heard the front door open. Silently she advanced to the top of the stairs leading to the first floor. The lights came on below and she saw him.

Anna stepped back and darted into the first bedroom in the hallway. The hall light came on. She stood with her back flat against the wall. Hurried footsteps passed the door. She held her breath and listened. *Shame on you. A gentleman would close the door to the bathroom even in an empty house.*

Silently Anna moved out into the hall and started down the stairs. She was almost to the bottom step when she heard the toilet flush.

Anna made her way quickly through the living room and then stopped and turned around. In the fireplace two burned out logs still glowed. *He turned on the lights before he passed the fireplace or he would have noticed the fire. Surely he will see it on his way back through this room and he will know that someone is in the house.*

Anna moved quickly to the kitchen. She opened the drawer to the cooking utensils. There was enough light coming into the kitchen from the living room to see and select the knife that Carol had called her butcher knife. She put her hand on it but did not lift it from the drawer. Anna froze. *I can't do it. I can't just kill him. He's done nothing to me.*

Anna closed the drawer without taking a knife. She silently walked from the kitchen and looked out the living room window. *The first grave is Amiee's. What will you do when you find it empty?*

She turned quickly and looked at the stairway. *Where is my intruder? He didn't come back downstairs. He must be checking the upstairs rooms. Will he find anything that will tell him that I am here?*

Too late Anna heard footsteps on the stairs. *There is no entry to the secret passageways on this floor. I must go to the basement.*

In the dark Anna hurried down the stairs only to trip and fall the last few. She scampered to her feet and listened. *Did he hear me?*

The light at the top of the stairs to the basement came on and Anna hurried over to the closet door beneath the stairs. His footsteps thundered down into the room. Anna stepped back against the wall as the rest of the lights in the basement came on.

Brad Marshall never looked her way. Instead, he walked directly across the room to the bar. He had his back to Anna as he pushed the bar aside. Anna opened the closet door and stepped inside. He didn't look her direction when he pushed the bar aside or when he lifted the trapdoor to the wine cellar. She closed the closet door and held the handle tightly. *This is just as I planned, but I have no weapon.*

Her fingers ached; she held the door handle so hard against the doorframe. If I turn the handle to open the passageway behind me, he will hear the click. But what if he saw me when he went down into the wine cellar?

A cold chill raced through Anna when she heard the slow deliberate footsteps approach the closet. She put her right foot against the doorframe and held tight to the handle. The footsteps passed. It was silent. *Too silent. You don't fool me. If you had left, I would have heard you going up the stairs.*

A feeling of warmth flood Anna's arms as she heard the footsteps on the stairs and her hands relaxed their iron grip on the door handle. She opened the door and entered the basement room.

In silence Anna walked up the stairs. *Is Jolie watching me? Has she made her way through the secret passageways to this room? She will see that I have failed her. Will she think that I have betrayed her too?*

Anna opened the front door and stepped out onto the porch. She could see now that both men were at the grave site. They had turned off the lights on the truck and only the short big man was digging by the light of the lantern. She looked up at the sky. Large dark clouds floated above. One was fast approaching the silver half-moon that hung high above. Anna stepped down the stairs from the porch to the yard. She moved to her left until the truck was between her and the lantern. Then she approached the graves. The cloud moved to cover the moon and she moved closer.

"Hey, Willy, that the fastest you can dig?"

"You could help, you know."

Anna watched as Willy alternated between using a pick to break up the dirt and the shovel to clear it away. She heard the pick strike something solid. Willy put the pick aside and reached for the shovel beside the grave.

Anna crouched and moved along the side of the pickup truck. Willie shoveled more quickly now. He moved around as his tool uncovered the top of the narrow coffin. Brad moved over to the edge of the grave but he made no effort to help.

Anna could see that Willy was not a fat man but a broad, powerfully built one. He put his shovel next to the pick and lifted one end of the coffin up out of the grave with one hand. A strong unceremonious whack from the pick and the latch flipped off.

"Why do that?" Brad protested. "They don't lock coffins."

Willy pried the lid off with the shovel and lay it aside. "What the Hell!"

Brad stepped forward to look down at the coffin.

"What now, Mister Marshall?"

"There are two more graves. I will bet that they are not both empty."

"Well, at least it wasn't buried very deep. Which one you want next?"

"Try this one next. Let's see if Jolie is home."

"Home? You don't believe in ghosts, do you?"

"A ghost would explain things." Brad turned and looked back toward the house.

Anna crouched beside the truck.

"Willy, you believe in ghosts?"

Willy laughed. "If I did, I wouldn't be digging up no grave. You know what we forgot?"

"What?"

"Something to drink. This is hard work."

"Here, take this. It's some brandy from the wine cellar. It's old but good enough for a night like tonight."

Anna held her breath as Brad walked past the pickup truck. She watched when he reached the house. One by one the lights went on in every window for a few seconds and then out again. Anna took a deep breath. "You didn't go back to the basement. You are searching the house again. You did notice the smoldering logs in the fireplace. You know someone is here but you said nothing to your lackey."

Anna backed away from the pickup truck. The moon suddenly broke out from behind the cloud and Anna froze. "I've got to get out of here but I can't move until it is darker."

She looked up at the heavens and for another dark blanket of clouds. There was one far to the west over the lake. Anna dropped to the ground and crawled under the pickup truck. She watched the dirt fly to the side of the second grave. The ground felt cold and damp. Anna pulled her arms under her. In a few minutes she was both cold and sleepy. She jumped when she saw the two feet march past her hiding place.

"Hell, it took you long enough," Willy complained.

Brad walked over to the grave and looked down. "Looks like you almost got it."

Willy climbed out of the grave and took the bottle from Brad's hand. With a clank of the shovel he broke off the top of the bottle, poured a little out into the dirt and lifted the bottle over his head. The liquid splashed his face as he drank without letting the broken glass touch his lips.

"Let's get it out," Brad ordered.

Willy handed the bottle back to Brad and leaned down. He pulled the end of the coffin up and pushed it to the side. Willy then knelt beside the long wooden box. He tried the latch but it wouldn't turn. He then bashed at the latch twice with his shovel before landing a solid blow. The latch shot off to the side. Willy flipped the lid open. "Hey, looks like she is home. Bring the lantern over here."

Anna scooted backward fearing Brad would see her when he came to get the lantern. Her head hit something metal. Holding her head she rolled behind the left front tire of the truck. Quickly she looked up to see if either of the men were coming her way.

Brad had ignored Willy's request for the lantern and was kneeling in the dirt at the foot of the coffin.

"What do you think, Mister Marshall? Is that a girl? It don't fill half the box."

"It is not Jolie," Brad replied.

"Hell no!" Willy laughed. "It's a monkey. Look at that damn head; the eyes are set way apart."

Willy reached into the coffin and picked up the skull. In Willy's large hand it looked small about the size of a grapefruit. "What we got here is a dwarf. A fucking dwarf! She was a fucking dwarf?"

With a loud metallic sound the end of the shovel struck Willy solid on the back of his head. The skull fell from his hand as Willy slowly collapsed into the first empty grave.

"You bastard! That man is my uncle."

Brad swung the shovel again and struck another blow. It hit the side of the grave before striking Willy's back. Willy did not move.

Anna's feet refused her command to run. She shook as she watched. Brad looked her way when he reached down to the dirt pile. He picked up the skull and placed it back in the coffin. For a long moment he knelt there looking at the remains in the coffin. "Ethan! It's got to be Ethan. She killed him. Damn! I know she did. The witch!"

Brad closed the lid to the coffin and walked to the last grave. He kicked aside the wooden marker that said Dorene and started digging.

Anna raised her head until her hair touched something above her. She started to inch her way out from under the truck.

Brad's voice barked. "No, you witch. I will not stop. There is but one more grave."

Astounded that he did not see her, Anna rose to her feet. He was removing his raincoat. She looked back at the mansion. *What can I do? Jolie is watching for sure. She knew they would find a man in her grave. This is my chance to run but what is in the last grave?*

Anna knelt silently beside the front bumper of the truck and watched. Brad picked up the shovel and began to dig. He soon worked up a sweat. He took off his jacket and folded it carefully and laid it by the lantern. Then he attacked the grave site with the pick. A cloud finally covered the moon and Anna felt more secure in the darkness.

Finally Anna noticed that Brad had put the pick aside and began to shovel more deliberately. She inched forward. *You must have reached the last coffin.*

Like the other two, this grave was a shallow one. When he had dug around sides of the coffin, Brad pried open the lid. "Ah! Ha! I found it."

He leaned over and pulled a old leather satchel from the coffin. Excitedly he moved to the lantern.

Anna peered around the left front tire of the truck. He pulled the satchel open and slowly took the items out. Each he lifted to the light for better viewing.

Anna felt the muscles in her neck stretch and she tried to see without moving further out of her hiding place. There was a small bag of probably coins, some papers and, last, a necklace. This Brad lifted to the light. Even in this dim light Anna knew it was the blue-diamond necklace.

Brad stood up and faced the house. Anna ducked down quickly. His voice reassured her that she was not seen.

"Jolie! JOLIE! YOU WITCH! I GOT IT! I FOUND THEM! HA! WHO GETS TO LAUGH NOW?"

Anna dropped to the ground. Just in time she rolled under the truck. She saw his shoes standing just inches away and heard the driver's door open.

Anna rolled over and lay still where she figured was the middle of the truck. *He can't drive forward because the graves are in the way. If he backs up, he will see me.*

Anna rolled over again to the far right side of the truck. The door slammed. *When he starts the engine, I must run for it.*

She turned her head to her left and saw his shoes. Brad returned to the last grave. He closed the lid and began to shovel dirt on top of the coffin.

Anna rolled back under the pickup truck. "He dose not have the satchel with him. I bet he put it in the truck."

She crawled under the truck to the driver's side and waited until he had finished filling the grave. When he stopped shoveling to take a drink of brandy, Anna moved just out from under the truck. She rose to her feet beside the driver's door. The driver's window was rolled up. She could see the satchel on the seat inside.

Anna put her hand on the door handle. She opened the door silently but as she did the dome light in the cab came on. In a flash, she reached inside, grabbed the satchel and ran for the house. She heard his cry of surprise. They were followed by his shouts of anger. Anna ran, desperately trying not to trip in the dark. When she reached the porch, she glanced back. He was following her but not running.

Anna rushed inside and closed the door. She bolted the door and then remembered that he had a key to the house.

Anna raced to the kitchen to get a weapon. Her hand pulled open the drawer but she just looked at the knives. "That's not my style."

She ran back to the living room and took the poker from the fireplace.

"Do you have the necklace?"

Anna turned to face the secret compartment behind the wall beside the fireplace. "Hell of a time for you to hide. He can't harm you."

"Bring me the necklace."

"That man is coming to kill me. I have got to get away."

"There is no better place to hide than in the dark."

Anna looked back at the front door. "Dark? Yes, darkness can be a friend."

Anna swung the poker from the fireplace and broke the bulbs in the chandelier above her. She moved quickly back to the living room. The sound of broken glass followed wherever she went. It was not until she reached the bedroom on the third floor and smashed the lamp beside the bed that she stopped and yelled, "Now come get me."

The door to the closet opened.

Anna held out the satchel. "Take your damn necklace and hide. We don't need to kill him."

"Keep the necklace. You need it to lure him to the wine cellar. When you do, I will kill him."

Setting the satchel on the bed, Anna turned and walked to the window. There she saw Brad Marshall with the lantern in one hand and the pick in the other, walking slowly toward the house.

Chapter 18

Anna raced down the stairs in the house. When she reached the first floor she saw a light on the porch and hurried across the living room. She had just reached the kitchen when she heard the front door open.

"Hello! I know you are here."

Anna stopped. *That basement door always squeaks. If I open it, he will hear me. Can I still beat him to the wine cellar? Did he leave the trapdoor open?*

"Whoever you are, come down. I want that necklace."

Anna held her breath and listened. *When I hear his footsteps going up those stairs, I can open the door to the basement.*

She heard footsteps but they came toward her, not away. She gripped the poker and crouched beside the door to the basement. The light from the lantern proceeded him into the kitchen. He moved directly to the counter beside the stove and jerked open one drawer after another. The was a moment of silence after Anna heard the drawer with the knives rattle open.

The light retreated back out of the kitchen. Anna rose to her feet. She heard a thump like a piece of wood hitting the floor. Silently she moved from her hiding place. *What is he up to now?*

Anna listened. The unmistakable sound of fresh kindling on a fire came to her ears. Even from here she could see the next room grow a little brighter. *He has restarted the fire in the fireplace.*

Anna put her hand on the knob to the basement door. His voice boomed from the other room.

"I am not coming up there after you. Either you come down or I will set this house ablaze."

The doorknob turned quickly. The door squeaked as she pulled it open. Anna raced down the stairs in the darkness. Once she reached the basement she moved more slowly. Her right hand held the satchel, her left swept the air searching for the trapdoor to the wine cellar. She heard his heavy footsteps coming down the stairs. The light from the lantern proceeded him. It was just enough for Anna to see the entrance to the wine cellar just a step or two away. She paused at the first step and looked back.

There he was. She hurried down the narrow stairs, but the panel on the back of the wine cellar was shut. She hadn't time to shut the trapdoor and pull the latch that would open the panel.

Anna turned as the light from the lantern shown into the stairway. She could not see his face, only that pale yellow light. She backed up until her head touched the back wall. The light moved to the top of the stairs. The wall behind Anna pushed forward. She dropped the satchel and stepped back into the secret passageway.

She heard a loud thud and suddenly he appeared just beyond the closing door. It stopped and then began to move open again. Anna grabbed the edge of the door and pulled. It started to close. She saw a set of fingers on the door just above her hand. *If I manage to pull the door closed, it will pinch my hands as well as his.*

A second set of fingers appeared just above the first and the door began to move away. Anna let go. The door jumped away from her. She heard a terrible scream, and the light in the wine cellar all but vanished.

She stuck her head around the door. There was no light but the glow on the mantel of the shattered lantern. Anna squinted and she made out the form of a man on the floor of the wine cellar. The dark handle of a butcher knife protruded from the pocket of his raincoat.

He moaned and he raised his head.

Anna reached down and grabbed the satchel with her left hand.

With a slow deliberate effort, the shadow of a man used both hands to pull the knife from his side.

Anna leaned down and with the fingers of her right hand crushed the glowing mantel. She lifted her burnt fingers to her lips then slowly stepped back into the darkness of the secret passageway. *I am safe for I know these tunnels even in this darkness.*

She moved slowly and carefully, feeling the walls as she went. *I will find the shaft that leads up to the first floor. I can hide here as long as he does not set the house aflame.*

Anna reached the pillar with the boards attached to form a ladder.

I need both hands to climb.

She turned to set the satchel down and saw the light. It was just a small spot of light like a penlight flashlight would produce. It swept the floor of the passageway in slowly painted short arcs of light.

Anna put her right hand on the highest board nailed to the round pine pillar. She tried to move silently but swiftly. She could not get a firm grip on the ladder with her left hand and still hold the satchel. The small narrow spot of light was coming closer.

She put the leather handle of the satchel in her teeth.

The small beam of light was on the bottom of the pine pillar. She started up the ladder. The light appeared like a spider just beside her head. Anna moved faster but her feet could not find the boards. She felt a hand on her left foot. "No! Help!"

The satchel fell and the hand let go. As fast as she could Anna ascended the ladder. She reached the next level. *From here I can enter the basement through the closet under the stairs. If I hurry, I can close the trap door to the wine cellar and trap him.*

Anna moved quickly down the narrow passageway and entered the closet. For a moment she listened at the door that led to the basement. *Where is he? Did he move quickly back down the passageway to the wine cellar? When I open this door, will I meet a madman with a bloody butcher knife? The longer I wait the more time he has to find his way back to the wine cellar.*

She turned the door handle and rushed out into the basement. She searched the air for the bar with her left hand as she moved quickly across the basement. *If I move too fast, I may fall down the stairs into the wine cellar. If I move too slowly, I will meet him coming up the stairs.*

The knuckles of her left hand hit the bar with a loud bang. She pulled her hand back. A voice came from just below where she stood.

"Stop, thief."

Anna froze and looked down at the darkness. Again she heard the voice.

"Monsieur Marshall, you are the thief. This belongs to Jolie."

Anna knelt down as she heard a second voice.

"Come here and I'll cut you to pieces, you little bitch."

Anna searched the floor with her hands until she found the trapdoor. Hurriedly she closed it. *Jolie, keep that man away just a little longer.*

Anna retraced her steps to the bar and began to push it back into the center of the room. *I hope this is over that trapdoor. I wonder what Jolie is up to now? Will she kill him as she said she would?*

She pushed the bar a little further toward the center of the room and then turned. For a moment Anna was confused in the dark. *Now which way are those stairs?*

She tried to walk in a straight line. *I should have reached the stairs by now. I must be going in the wrong direction.*

She turned and took a few steps to her right. Where are those stairs?

She heard a sudden grating noise behind her. *He is trying to open the trapdoor to the wine cellar. If I didn't move the bar all the way over the trapdoor, he will succeed.*

Anne turned her back and walked directly away from the sound. She had just put her right hand in front of her when her fingers touched the wall. Anna moved to her left, feeling along the wall as she did. Her right foot touched the bottom step. She took a deep breath and raced up the stairs. The light in the kitchen was so welcome that tears came to her eyes.

She ran on through the kitchen and the living room and out on to the porch. A large hand grabbed her arm as the front door slammed shut.

"Where is he?"

Anna tried to pull away, but the man jerked her off her feet and pulled her face up to his. There was dried blood on the big round face. His eyes looked like red tennis balls. His mouth opened like a square trap. "Where is he?"

"He's in the wine cellar." Anna felt her body go limp in his hand.

He tossed her aside and entered the house.

She fell down the stairs to the porch. Without looking back she crawled to her feet and started to run.

Chapter 19

Jolie waited until Brad Marshall had reached the steps in the wine cellar. He paused when he heard the bar above being dragged across the floor. She heard him swear. “Damn you, bitch. You tried to trap me here. Too slow. I can still get out.”

Jolie waited until the small yellow dot of a light had reached the top of the stairs. In the dimming light she saw him set the satchel down and reach up with his left hand.

“Monsieur Marshall, I will take this.”

Jolie picked up the satchel, just as he turned quickly in the dark. Jolie stepped back.

“Stop, thief.”

“Monsieur Marshall, you are the thief. This belongs to Jolie.”

The small dot of yellow light searched the floor until it reached the black lace of her gown. As the light traced it until it found the satchel. Jolie stepped backwards but he acted too quickly. The butcher knife cut through the lace gown. The force of his blow knocked the satchel from her hand. In the dark he held the knife in front of him. “Come here and I’ll cut you to pieces, you little bitch.”

The little dot of light found Jolie’s eyes just as his foot brushed against the satchel. He reached down with the hand that held the knife and picked up the satchel. The small pen light traced its way to the darkness where her face should have been. Brad retreated.

Jolie crawled a short distance down the passageway in the darkness. She closed her eyes and relied on her memory and her fingers to tell her where she was. Slowly coming to her feet, she started back down the passageway toward the wine cellar. This time she held her silver dagger tightly in her right hand.

At the back panel of the wine cellar that was also the entrance from the passageways, she paused. He was halfway up the stairs pounding on the trapdoor above. Jolie turned. “Anna did it. She pushed the bar over the entrance. He is trapped.”

Jolie gently pulled on the panel that was the back wall to the wine cellar. “Fool, you are so intent in escaping in that direction you failed to see the rest of the trap."

Jolie made her way silently down the secret passageway to the pillar that served as a ladder to the next floor. As she climbed slowly to the next level, she heard heavy footsteps on the stairs to the basement. "Who is that?"

Jolie stopped at the basement level and made her way silently and slowly to the closet in the basement. The moment she entered the closet she could hear Brad Marshall's muffled cries.

"Help! Down here! Help!"

Jolie opened the closet door. In the darkness she could see nothing, but she could smell someone. She could also hear the scraping sound of the heavy wooden bar being moved. *No. Don't set him free.*

"Oh! Thank God!"

Jolie opened the door to the closet wide. *There are two of them, but I still have my dagger.*

Jolie started to move forward when she heard a sudden crash and a yell.

"You son of a bitch. I'm going to kill you, Marshall."

"Willy, don't please. Don't!"

"Hell! What were you going to do? Leave me in that grave?"

"No. Willy, it wasn't me. Help me out of here. I'll explain everything."

"I don't trust you. Give me the keys to the truck first."

Jolie stepped back and feeling her way along the wall found the stairs leading to the kitchen. *I will leave these two. One will surely kill the other and I will be waiting when the winner tries to leave.*

As Jolie started up the stairs, she heard Brad Marshall's voice again.

"OK! Willy, here's the keys. Just let me out of here. OK! Let me out?"

Jolie shook her head. "Only a fool would trust a man in the dark with a butcher knife."

The primal scream in the dark told Jolie that the man had done just that. She didn't stop to listen to the battle below but went silently to wait in the living room near the front door.

In the distance Jolie could hear the wail of a siren. She looked out the window. The pickup truck was still parked down by the carriage house. The moon was lost in the tall trees but still a little patch of light shown on the lone open grave. The clamor of footsteps came so fast that Jolie had hardly time to turn before the big cow of a man came through the room. She stepped back from the window. He crashed into the front door, jerked it open and was gone.

Jolie watched as he ran across the yard to the pickup truck. She heard the engine roar. The lights came on just as the truck began to back up. *He didn't have the satchel. I could not have stopped him anyway.*

Softer footsteps made their way across the kitchen. Jolie turned to face that direction. She held her silver dagger at ready.

In the dim light of the fireplace Jolie saw the bent form of a man. He dragged his right leg as he came closer. Jolie stepped forward. Just as his shadow entered the living room she stepped back behind the open front door. *An open door - an invitation to escape, the final trap.*

Jolie tracked his path across the room by the sound of the march of his left shoe. The sirens in the distance became a high-pitched scream just outside the door. Bright red and white lights flashed through the window. Jolie shoved hard on the door. The man fell, his head making a loud thump on the floor. In a flash she knelt beside him, her dagger at his throat. "Now who has won? You do not steal from Jolie."

The sirens outside came to a sudden stop. Jolie reached in the satchel, her fingers found the necklace. "I give you your life Monsieur Marshall which is more than your father did for me."

On the porch she could hear men yelling.

"Police. Open the door."

Jolie moved quickly to the stairs. She had just started up when the front door burst open.

Chapter 20

The Sunday following the attack on the house in Harrison, Father David visited Anna Holmes and her family at their home.

"I must apologize for my brother's actions. He started with the incorrect premise that there was something of value buried in one of the graves, namely a blue-diamond necklace. In his efforts to retrieve it, he broke several laws and endangered you."

"An apology ain't enough," Mr. Holmes said. He shook his head slowly. "That man should be put in jail. He attacked my daughter."

Father David nodded. "He will admit to illegal entry and to menacing. He never struck your daughter. Now I know that does not seem like enough to you. Let me make you a proposal to end this."

"Hell no. We ain't making no deal. I would rather let the courts decide," Mr. Holmes declared. "Let's see if a jury thinks it was just menacing."

"Pa, let's hear what Father David has to say." Anna walked across the room to her father's side. "I'll do whatever you think is best."

Mr. Holmes put his arm around Anna's shoulders. "Okay, what's your deal?"

Father David again nodded. "First we will pay Mrs. Potter for any damage done to her property. Second we will pay for any medical bills that Anna might incur."

"I'm fine."

Father David shook his head. "You should have a complete physical and a psychological exam as well. We want to know now so that any problems that arise later can be accounted for. Now I don't mean that you have any problems. What I mean you should seek counseling if, for example, you have recurring dreams of the events of that night."

Anna smiled.

"Now, the reason for my seeking an out-of-court settlement in exchange for you dropping charges of assault are these. The family is prominent in Spokane and we do not wish any scandals. I ask you to consider the rest of our family in this regard. There have been problems in the past and we do not wish to give the press reasons to revisit those past indiscretions."

Anna looked up at her father. He was shaking his head as he listened.

"There is also my brother. He has his faults but he is quite good at running a bank. He cannot remain president of the bank without my support. I have a great deal of influence on the board of directors. I will keep him in check."

Father David smiled. "Brad has never been convicted of a crime. Not even a parking violation. So it is not likely that in any case he would get anything more than a fine if he were convicted. And there is a chance he would not be convicted of any crime. He has retained a prestigious law firm for his defense."

"We have a district attorney with a good record for getting convictions." Mr. Holmes grinned. "Especially for people from Washington who come down here and stir things up."

Father David nodded. "I wish to avoid all that. In a criminal trial, even if convicted, my brother would get only a fine. I assure you his lawyers will see to that. You will have to file in civil court for any punitive damages. There is where his new law firm has the advantage. On the other hand, if you drop your charge of assault, tomorrow I will establish a scholarship fund at the bank in your name. Now the cost of a year at the state university will be about $5,000."

Anna clutched her father's arm and Father David continued.

"Four years would be $20,000."

Anna looked up at her father's face. He was shaking his head slowly. "Now that's quite an offer. Let me discuss this with my wife and of course with Anna."

Father David looked around the room. "You have by my count six daughters. Is that right?"

"Yes sir."

"One hundred and twenty thousand dollars will be transferred to a trust account in your name tomorrow."

Anna raised her hand. "Wait a minute. Did your brother agree to all this? Or will his lawyers have another deal, like charging me with something."

Father David raised his hands and nodded his gray head. "I will have the lawyer at the bank draw up the out-of-court settlement. In it, you will agree not to file for punitive damages against my brother and you will drop your charge of assault in criminal court. This agreement we will present in writing to your lawyer and the county attorney for review. The money will be transferred Monday but I will not tell you the account until you agree to the settlement."

Mr. Holmes raised his shoulders. "I guess I have to find a lawyer."

"Don't worry, Pa. I bet Judge Parker will look the agreement over for us. She will want to know what it says anyway."

Anna followed Father David out to his limousine. "How is your brother?"

"He's doing better. They are keeping him in the hospital to check for infection. Those knife wounds are very deep."

"I never stabbed him."

"He claims you did."

"He fell back on the knife when he was chasing me."

The driver for Father David's limo came back to open the door for him.

After Father David was seated in the limousine, Anna held the door open and asked, "How do I know that your brother won't send someone else after that blue-diamond necklace?"

Father David smiled. "I pointed out to Brad that he has no claim to the necklace. It belonged to my mother, not his. When she died, she left all her fortunes to me; that included not only her stock in the bank but also her jewelry. You see the house in Harrison was not my father's first indiscretion. In fact it was Mother's retreat. It was not until after she died that the nature of the house changed."

"What if the necklace is found?"

Father David sat back deep into the leather seat. "Until last week, I thought Frank had found it. I still do not understand how he painted it into the portrait of Jolie. If the necklace is found in the house or anywhere on the property of Mrs. Potter then she will have first claim. However, if it were found in the grave as my brother claims, that would be one for the courts to sort out. You don't have the necklace, do you?"

Anna shook her head. "Jolie has the necklace."

Father David shook his head. "I don't believe that the ghost of Jolie haunts this house?"

"Believe what you wish, but Frank saw her. I've seen her and I have spoken to her. Ask your brother. I bet at least one of those stab wounds came from Jolie's dagger."

"I will ask him just that."

Frank took the packet of letters and moved to the back of the group of soldiers. Mail call was like this; either you got nothing or you got a bunch. He separated the junk mail and tore it up and then counted the letters. There were nine in all, one each from Aunt Connie and D. Marshall S.J., and seven from the universities he had written; none were from Anna.

The company was headed for Saigon on "normal rotation." He and almost half the company would be going home. Their replacements were already beginning to arrive. In a few weeks the company would be back at full strength and headed back to the delta.

Despite the heat, David felt a chill. *Damn! I'd better not be getting malaria. It is my time to go home.* He half squatted in the shade of a tree and began to read.

If he got back, he would have his choice of graduate schools to attend, but only one offered him a financial support in the form of a teaching assistance job.

"One is better than none," David said.

He read his aunt's letter next. She told of his grandmother falling at the mansion and being taken to the hospital in Coeur d'Alene. Last David opened the letter from Father David. He read it, slowly; then, in disbelief, he read it a second and third time, especially the last two pages.

My brother has agreed to drop his charges against Anna. I am sure a DNA test will conclude that the body in Jolie's grave is indeed that of my Uncle Ethan. This summer after the legal matters are settled, I will have the body moved to the family burial plots.

Both Anna Holmes and my brother Brad claim to have seen Jolie in the mansion. You lived in that house for most of the summer before you left for Vietnam. Did you encounter any unusual things in the house? Did you hear or see anything that would lead you to think that Jolie, in spirit, was present? I am especially interested in the painting you did of Jolie. What prompted you to add a blue-diamond necklace to the portrait? Your reply will be kept in the utmost confidence.

"Hey Potter!"

"Yeah!" Frank called back.

"You left too soon. Got some more mail."

David jumped to his feet. The green horizon blinked and then rose to greet him like a wave at the ocean. David pushed hard against the wall as it crashed around him but it just kept moving. The green wave pulled him forward but something was pulling him back and then suddenly all was darkness.

It was a week later when Frank boarded the plane with assistance from a medic. His lost letters hadn't caught up with him at the hospital, and they would never find him now. He remembered the name Father David Marshall S.J. and the question. If he ever got off this medication, he'd have to write. If only he could remember the name of the school that had offered him financial assistance.

Anna didn't wait. The day her father agreed to the out-of-court settlement she wrote to the University of Idaho. She told her father that she would rather go to a school further away but he would not consent to that.

That spring Carol Potter moved back to live in the house in Harrison. Judge Parker complained about the arrangement but Carol was walking without the support of a cane now. Anna lived at home but was a frequent visitor to the house in Harrison.

"Have you heard that Frank is going to be released early by the Army?" Carol asked.

"I got a letter Friday. When he was being treated for malaria, they discovered that he had a heart mummer. I could have told them he had a weak heart."

"Then you know he'll be here next week. I can't wait to see him. Boy, will you have a story to tell."

Anna sat quietly and stared at the painting of Jolie on the wall.

"What are you thinking?" Carol asked.

"I am going to the University of Idaho in the fall. What is Frank going to do?"

Chapter 21

The first Monday in June, Frank was released from active duty. He stopped on the way to the airport and changed into his civilian clothes. Despite his casual shirt and pants, the short haircut and clean-shaved face identified him as part of the military. At the airport in San Diego, one group of young men with long hair mocked him with the peace sign; another group gave him a one-finger salute as he passed. The young woman at the gate took his ticket and gave him a boarding pass. “Have a nice flight.”

Frank smiled but she had already turned her attention to the next customer in line. At the airport in Spokane the people were a little more friendly. As he had requested, his aunt Connie had left the old pickup truck in the long term parking area. She and his grandmother would be waiting for him in Harrison.

He stopped several times on the drive down. The lake looked so much bluer, the sky so much clearer. He rolled down the window and let the cool air buffet his face.

By the time he reached Harrison the crimson sky had faded to a deep blue. In town the buildings looked the same, but the street looked wider. Frank pulled his truck to the curb in front of the city park as the parking spots nearer the restaurant were all taken. He rehearsed his little speech once more before he got out of the truck. He didn’t want to sound too corny or too casual. It was cooling off quickly and he pulled on his new green jacket. The present he had brought Anna seemed too little and too big at the same time. He tried to hide it under his jacket, but this felt bulky so he put it back in the truck and slammed the door.

“Hi!”

Frank turned to see her standing on the walk beside the truck. She looked different, taller, slimmer, older, sexier, and so simply beautiful.

“Welcome home.” She took a step down from the curb. He took a step forward.

"Was that for me?" she asked.

Frank looked across the hood of the truck at the present he had tossed inside. Her arms encircled his waist and Frank leaned down. It was a soft kiss, a long kiss, one that said everything he could not find words to say.

When they drove up the hill, Frank stopped to say hello to Anna's parents. Her mother and father seemed extremely quiet, while her sisters all talked at once.

He got a second welcome when they drove to the mansion. His aunt Connie and his grandmother, Carol, had a late dinner waiting for him. David ate and talked about his plans throughout the meal. After dinner he excused himself to walk Anna back home.

"So you're going to Montana?" Anna said as they walked arm in arm.

"I won't go until the fall. It's a good thing. I have to learn to paint all over again. Guess I'll spend the summer here in Harrison just painting."

"I am going to college too. I got accepted at the University of Idaho. So I'll only be here for the summer."

"Why don't you go to Montana with me?"

"My father wouldn't like that."

"Why not?"

"You know why not. He thinks you are out to get me. He wants me to finish college."

"He's a smart man. I wonder what he thinks the boys at Idaho will try? At least you know me."

"Do we really know each other, Frank?"

They stopped just up the road from the house. David held her tight. "Know you? I've dreamed of you ever since I left."

"Really?"

"Well, ever since I started making plans to return. I don't want to take you home. Let's go back to the mansion."

"With your aunt and grandmother?"

"It's better than five sisters watching us; besides they go to bed early."

Anna leaned her head against his chest. “Do you know I slept in Jolie’s room while you were gone?”

“Well, that’s just what I had in mind.”

“I know what you have in mind. Not tonight.”

“When?”

Frank looked down at her and held her just a little tighter. “Soon, Frank. Soon. Your aunt goes to Coeur d’Alene every Wednesday, and she usually stays overnight. Can you wait that long?”

“It won’t be easy.”

“It won’t be easy for me either.”

Wednesday finally arrived and Frank hurried through the rain down into town. He rushed into the café and took the last stool at the end of the counter. Anna blushed when she came down to the counter caring a coffee pot in one hand and a menu in the other.

“Guess what?” Frank whispered. “She left.”

“I told you she would,” Anna replied. She filled his coffee cup.

“They both left. They won’t be back until tomorrow night,” Frank said.

“Shhh! Not so loud,” Anna replied. She leaned over and kissed his cheek before turning and walking away.

Frank studied her figure as she moved across the room. Her black slacks fit tighter than her blue jeans ever had. The white blouse was tailored cotton that fit snug at the shoulders. Anna seemed to take forever making the rounds as she refilled the coffee cups at the four tables. He could see the straps to her bra under the back of her blouse. At the last table she turned suddenly as if she felt the heat of his stare. All but the top button of the blouse were fastened. The pockets bulged a little, like patches over her breasts. She walked quickly behind the counter and on into the kitchen. Frank took a long sip of the blistering hot coffee.

“Let’s go.”

He looked up to see her standing by his chair, her jacket on and her purse in hand. They hurried to the truck and drove quickly up the hill.

At the mansion they hurried in from the rain and continued at that hurried pace through the house. They didn't stop on the first floor but went straight for the bedroom on the third floor. Frank tossed his jacket on the floor. She tossed hers on top of his. He cursed his shoes, wishing he had western boots that quickly slipped off. By the time he got his pants down she was undoing the snaps on her bra. Their arms encircled each other as they rolled onto the bed without bothering to pull down the covers. The bed shook and the bed springs sang. It even marched a short distance across the floor. Time seemed suspended as they rested, talked, and made love a second time.

Later when Frank awoke, he rose to open the window. Anna looked up and smiled but said nothing. Down below Frank saw a black limousine pulling slowly up the muddy road past the carriage house.

"Now who in the hell is that?" Frank mumbled.

Anna came to the window and look out as the car drew nearer.

"Guess we'd better get dressed," she said. Her smile turned to a dimpled grin. "Don't look so sad. Whoever it is won't stay and your aunt and Carol will be gone until tomorrow."

"Stay here," Frank said. "I'll go see who it is."

Chapter 22

Despite Frank's hurrying to get dressed, the visitor had to wait a few minutes before Frank came to the door.

"Good morning, Frank," Father David said. "May I come in?"

"Sure."

The old priest walked slowly, the silver cane in his right hand used for only token support. He paused to admire the old piano, then the paintings on the wall. "I drove up here myself. I heard that your grandmother would be in Coeur d'Alene today. What I want to do does not concern her. Say, I hope that I am not interrupting anything?"

"Not really. What did you want?" David asked.

"I believe I have resolved the ghost problem, but I need your help. Can we talk privately? Perhaps a walk down to the grave site?"

"I left my jacket upstairs."

"Well, it's raining anyway. I noticed that the three grave markers are still there. Have you heard the story of my brother's visit here?"

"Anna told me about it in a letter. We haven't talked about it since I got back."

"You haven't? Well, Brad claims that he took a satchel from Jolie's grave. It contained among other things a necklace. He further claims that the necklace is the same one that belonged to my mother. In other words, it looks exactly like the one you painted into Jolie's portrait. Now I ask you, Frank, did you find the necklace?"

"No, Father. I never found a necklace in this house and I never dug up any of those graves."

Both eyebrows on Father David's face rose considerably and then settled down as a smile spread across his face. "But you did tell me that you saw Jolie here in this house?"

"That's true. It was late at night. There was a storm that night. It was the night that I finished painting Jolie's portrait."

Father David nodded slowly, "Anna, too, claims to have seen Jolie in this house."

"Yes, she told me about that."

He smiled and asked. "Is Anna here?"

"Yes," Frank replied hoping he wasn't blushing. "She's upstairs."

"Good, let's not disturb her. It's the basement I wanted to see."

Frank led the way, switching the lights as he went. Father David looked around, walked to the bar, then studied the floor. "The wine cellar is under here. Can you move the bar?"

"It is?" Frank said.

"Surely Anna told you of the bar and the wine cellar?"

"Anna! Oh yes, she said something about my grandmother falling down the stairs."

"Frank, move the bar. I want to see it."

At Father David's direction Frank slid the bar aside and opened the door to the wine cellar. Frank marveled that there were still some bottles left along the wall below. "I never knew this was here."

"This is the story, though I am not sure of all of it. But it's the best I can do." The little priest studied the wine cellar below. "My Uncle Ethan built this house and in it he built a series of secret passageways. He was himself a dwarf so the passageways he built were small. Somehow Jolie - you do know about my father's mistress - anyway she found out about them."

Frank felt his eyes widen. Here a priest was talking about his father having a mistress. No condemnation, no lecture. The priest continued as he started down the first step into the wine cellar.

"Ethan was sent to Harrison to get rid of the women after my father remarried. Something went wrong and he was killed. By some strange coincidence the big fire on the Harrison waterfront broke out the next day and Jolie used the fire as a cover. She buried Ethan but had the grave markers carry her name and the names of her two cousins who also lived here. Not all went as she planned. My uncles Samuel and David came to see what damage the fire had done. Now the rest is speculation. Jolie must have hidden in the passageway. Not knowing she was there, Samuel moved the bar over the trapdoor. That locked her inside. Jolie died trapped in this house. No one can live for fifty years without food and water. Now Anna claims, and you did too, that the ghost of Jolie haunts this house. In fact you said you think you saw her when you were doing that portrait?"

Frank followed Father David down into the wine cellar. "Yes, I could have. There was a storm that night. I don't know what I saw but that was when I put the necklace in the portrait."

"That's part of the problem. Our minds try to find a logical reason for whatever we see. A very fervent religious Christian may see the face of Jesus in the light from a stained glass window; you would probably see the dust in the air colored by the light. If for a second it formed an image, it would be the face of a pretty girl, perhaps Anna's face. Don't laugh. It has happened to me more than once."

"But Father, Anna saw her too. Maybe this house is haunted?"

"Come now, your aunt told me you said just that. Don't let me change your impression. Too many others have seen her. The spirit of Jolie is present here. Which reminds me, I brought the diary. Would you give it back to Anna?"

"Thank you, Father. I hope you found it enlightening."

Both Frank and Father David looked up to see Anna standing above them. Frank started up the stairs but Anna was coming down so he stepped aside and offered her his hand for support.

"Good, I am glad that you are here. I was just about to tell Frank that I believe the spirit of Jolie is sheltered in this house, because - the remains of her body lie here also. Now Frank is too big to have explored these passageways, but you are of much shorter statue. Have you been in there?"

"Yes," Anna said. "I've been everywhere."

"Good. You can save me some time looking around. Are Jolie's remains in there?"

Frank reached up as Anna reached the bottom step. He offered her his hand. She took it briefly and then stepped onto the floor of the wine cellar.

Anna looked directly at Father David. "Jolie is still in this house."

"Anna, I have concluded that because her physical remains are here that you have perceived her spirit here too. I want you to help me remove Jolie's remains."

"Why?"

"I wish to put them in a proper grave and give her a Christian burial."

Anna walked past the priest to the far wall of the wine cellar. She turned and glanced up at Frank, then back at the priest. "Why not leave her here?"

"I told you. I want to give her a Christian burial. That should put an end to any more images of her in the house."

Anna folded her arms and replied, "How could you bury a harlot in a public cemetery? No one would dare bury their kin in the adjoining plot."

Frank rolled his eyes. This was no way to speak to a priest. Anna had changed; she was certainly not the shy girl he had left two years ago.

"You are correct," Father David replied. "Here in the passageways beneath an old house is not a proper last place. I have received Mrs. Potter's permission to bury Jolie's remains down by the carriage house. I would of course give her a Catholic funeral first."

"Why? After all these years, why change anything now?" Anna protested.

Father David shook his head. "Because I wish to put and end to the notion that the house is haunted. Once everyone knows that she is buried in the grave out there I don't think we'll have any more sightings here in the house."

Anna stepped closer to the Father David. "Is that what Catholics believe? No heaven? No hell? The spirit just follows the dead body until it is properly buried?"

Frank swallowed hard. Father David smiled as he answered.

"No, at least it's not what you will hear from the pulpit." His eyes and his voice softened. "We believe in a life after death, a heaven and a hell. Some will include a purgatory, a temporary hell if you wish. I am an old man with only a few years to live, when I die and that may be soon, I will more clearly understand these things. The living must simply believe."

Anna shook her head, “Reverend John says that God is forgiving. He would welcome her into heaven and not leave her here in this darkness. Somehow she must not be really dead?”

“I know,” Frank said, his voice a little louder than either of theirs. They both turned to look at him. He stammered, “She died but she didn’t go to heaven or hell; she stayed here. She’s waiting for someone to rescue her.”

Anna smiled but shook her head. “Frank, you are so romantic.” She took his hand. “If she were dead, God would take her to heaven. He wouldn’t leave her imprisoned here for fifty years. What if the rescuer never comes?”

Father David held up his hand. “This is just my point. You, Anna, are a beautiful woman, and you look a little like Jolie. For Frank to see you in a flash of lightning does not surprise me. You are both young and romantic. That is why you saw Jolie. Now after her body is removed and given a proper burial all this will end.”

“But what of your brother?” Anna protested. “Did he too not see Jolie?”

“He told me that he heard a voice. At the time he was in the dark in this passageway. Correct me if I am wrong. Each time you heard her you were in the dark of the same passageway. Both of you were very concerned with finding your way out.”

Anna shook her head, “No. That was only the first time I met Jolie. There were other times.”

She leaned back against the wall of the wine cellar. “I think we should quit arguing and let you see for yourself. Her remains are on this the lowest level of the passageways. If you would dare go into the passageway, you will find Jolie. The tunnel is big enough at this level for you to enter. She’s down there. Put your offer of a Christian burial to her, but remember she stabbed your brother.”

“My foolish brother was trying to steal her necklace.”

“Then he did see her?” Anna proclaimed.

“He said that he saw but a black robe and a silver dagger. In the darkness that would frighten anyone.” He smiled. “It could have been you that he saw.”

"I'll go with you," Frank offered.

"No," Anna said. "She would kill you both. She has the necklace. She won't let you take it away. Father I fear that you will meet with the same fate as your brother."

Father David shook his head slowly. "I know that won't happen. If the necklace is there, it will be buried with her."

"What if she doesn't believe you? What if she thinks that you are just out to steal that necklace like your brother did?" Anna's voice rose as she spoke.

Father David took a candle from his coat pocket. "She will believe me. You see, I gave her the necklace."

"Liar, her lover gave her that necklace," Anna countered. "It's in her diary. Her lover."

Frank felt his jaw drop. *How can Anna speak like that to a priest?*

Father David nodded his head as he lit the candle. "I, too, have read her diary. Jolie had many lovers. She did not say who gave her the necklace. It was mine, given to me by my mother and I choose to give it to Jolie. I would never take it from her. How do we enter the passageway?"

"Oh hell! Step aside," Anna said. She showed Frank the latch he would have to pull once he had closed the door above them.

"Hey, we'll need a flashlight. That little candle will never do," Frank argued as he closed the first of the doors above.

"It is a holy candle. It is just the proper source of light." The old priest blessed himself as the far corner of the wall moved a little toward them. Anna reached out and pulled it the rest of the way open.

"Thank you," Father David said. He stepped forward into the passageway.

Frank hit his head as he tried to follow. The priest quickly disappeared into the darkness.

With Father David departed the candle, the only source of light in the wine cellar. Frank heard Anna issued directions.

"She is just down the passageway to the right. Go all the way to the end. It looks like no more than an old blanket rolled up. That is where she stays during the day time; by night she roams the house.

Are you sure you don't want me to go with you?"

"No, you and Frank can stay there. I won't be long."

Frank listened intently to the sound of Father David's short footsteps until he could no longer hear them. Frank reached out in the darkness and pulled Anna close to him. The sound of the priest's voice in prayer was the only sound now. Frank listened as Father David asked God to forgive Jolie for her failures and especially for leading two others into following her ways. Frank turned to Anna when he heard a second voice.

"Hypercritical prêtre! Who are you to ask mercy for me? If you had the nerve, you would have followed in your father's footsteps. Now you ask that I be forgiven; what of you?"

Father David's voice continued in prayer.

"I was here fifty years. I hungered for someone. That's why I didn't kill the boy who came here to paint. He spoke. After all that time, I finally heard a voice. He spoke my name. Oh my God, how I missed that! Now he has finally returned and you wish to drag me away. Do you know how long I waited for you to return and you came not?"

Frank now heard Father David saying the Lord's prayer.

"And what of that necklace! Did you send your uncle to take it back?"

Again Father David spoke her name and called on God to forgive her for leading Amiee and Dorene astray.

"You are still the boy. The one who ran from life afraid to admit he loved his father's mistress. Why didn't you come back for me?"

The priest's voice continued as if he had heard nothing. "She is not alone in her sin. I and others have sent her to the life she led. God grant that I may now in some way atone for our sin."

"Too late. Too late. I am condemned to dwell here forever. I was a fool. I waited for you to come and you never came."

Frank felt Anna holding him, her head laid heavy against his chest. "Does he not hear her? Can he not see her?"

Frank replied was a whisper. "I bet he has his eyes closed. Most priests do that when they pray. As for hearing her, his own voice is all he hears now."

Anna's arms slipped from around Frank and she stepped forward into the darkness. Frank reached out as she passed. "Wait."

Frank tried to follow only to hit his head on the doorframe that led into the passageway. Anna was gone and he stood there alone. He listened, trying to hear her footsteps in the dark. But he heard only Father David's voice in prayer. Before the prayer stopped, he felt Anna's hand in his again.

The priest's voice changed suddenly. "Anna? I lost my light. Anna?"

Frank felt Anna grip his arm. "Don't say a word," she whispered.

"Anna? Frank? The blessed candle went out. Where are you?"

"Monsieur David, you are so like a little boy. Don't tremble so; Jolie will help you."

"Anna?"

"No, Monsieur, I am Jolie. You finally came for me, but you came too late. Go now. Go. I will thank God that you came but now you must go. I will show you the way."

"Frank," Anna whispered. "Reach up and open the door above. Quickly."

Frank felt the ceiling until he found the latch, turned it and pushed up. Light entered the wine cellar like a curtain. Frank turned to see Father David standing at the passageway door. He stepped inside and Anna closed the panel behind him. They said nothing as they ascended the stairs into the basement. Frank leaned back to help Father David up the stairs. A hand gripped Frank's shoulder and yanked him backwards. Like a sack of potatoes he was tossed across the room.

"You two. Come on up," the two men ordered.

Frank scrambled to his feet. Both of the men outweighed him by perhaps a hundred pounds. Together he didn't stand a chance. Father David and Anna climbed the stairs into the room.

"Upstairs," was the next order. With one of the twin bull-like-men leading the way and the other following, they all went upstairs to the living room. Not even Father David protested.

Anna stood beside Frank and Father David just between the love seat and the fireplace. The two men stood ten feet away whispering to each other.

"Double bonus. What of him? Same treatment. What of her? Same treatment. She's hot. Another bonus. Me first."

Frank shot a glance at Father David. He was either still in shock from his meeting with Jolie or praying for God's help. If they were going to do anything, it had best be now. Frank sprang straight at the two men. They reacted alike. Two blows sent Frank crashing to the floor. He shook his head expecting another fist or foot but none came.

"Get her."

Frank looked up to see the twin bulls bump into each other as they ran to block Anna's path to the front door. She turned at the hall and raced up the stairs. The bulls hurried off in pursuit. Frank jumped to his feet and joined the chase.

By the time she reached the top floor Anna was several seconds ahead of the men. She slammed the door to her room and headed for the closet. Hearing the thunder of footsteps in the hall she figured it was too late to slip into the passageway. She shut the closet door and dashed to the bed.

The door behind Anna burst open just as her hand found the cold steel of the crowbar on the floor under the bed. The first bull, unable to check his speed, crashed into the bed, his huge left hand reaching out for her as he fell. Turning the steel bar in her hand as she swung Anna drove the claw into the bull's forehead. With a scream he rolled aside to the floor.

Anna yanked the bar loose only to have a large hand snatch it from her. The second bull jerked her to her feet and tossed her across the bed. For a moment he glanced down at his twin who was trying to struggle to his feet. At the sound of footsteps in the hall, the standing bull turned with the crowbar in his right hand. Anna stood up on the bed and hit the bull in his face with the only weapon she had at hand - a pillow. Frank was running at full speed but with a pillow in his face the bull never saw him until impact. The two crashed across the room and through the window.

Anna jumped from the bed and looked down. A meaty hand pulled her back. He looked like a monster, blood was pouring down his face from the hole in his forehead, his eyes were big as pool-balls, and his mouth was open wide in a scream that never came.

With one hand he slammed her to the bed. The second hand formed a fist that he raised high above her. Anna closed her eyes. The blow never came but a crashing sound did. She looked up to see Father David. For a moment his body just stood against the closet door; then he slid to the floor. The door to the closet opened pushing him aside as he fell. A monster hand twisted Anna's face to look up at his. Blood fell like rain on her face and pain jetted through her jaw. Despite the trauma she heard a high-pitched scream, the hand released her. She opened her eyes at the sound of the loud crash that followed.

The stillness was more frightening than the sound. Anna's eyes hurt; they opened so wide to search the room as she raised her head. The bull was nowhere to be seen. She sat up in bed. There was Father David kneeling at the closet door. Anna jerked her head around expecting to see one of the bulls at the other side of the bed. He was there all right, laying face down with a silver dagger protruding from the back of his neck.

Anna stepped over him and went to the window. On the ground below was the other bull. He was laying still looking up into the sky. Beside him Frank was trying to struggle to his feet.

"Don't move," Anna called. "I'm coming down."

At the doorway she paused and looked back at Father David. That is when she saw Jolie's black lace gown pull back into the closet. She heard the double click as the closet door pulled shut.

Chapter 23

Frank spent only a day in the hospital in Coeur d'Alene before being released. He had held tight to his adversary and landed on top of him when they hit the ground. This saved Frank's life but resulted in a broken neck for the other man. The attacker and his twin brother were identified as members of a Spokane motorcycle gang. Robbery was the likely motive for their attack, the Spokane newspapers reported.

But newspapers from Spokane to Boise had a field day, each trying to outdo the other in speculating on the identity the corpse found by police dogs in a hidden passageway in the basement of the house in Harrison. The story circulated that she had lived in the house for years without anyone in town knowing she was there.

"He may be a priest," Mr. Holmes declared to his daughters. "But it was his house and I just won't believe he didn't know the woman."

"You're right, Father," Anna replied. "No doubt they knew each other well. Did you know that Father David has arranged for her to be buried here in the grave that was marked Jolie. What do you think of that?"

"I think if I were you, I would have nothing further to do with any of those Potters."

"Now just you hold on," Anna's mother said. "If you were Frank Potter, just what would you do?"

Anna folded her arms across her chest and smiled at her father. He took a deep breath, glanced at Anna, then back at his wife. "Woman, you know very well what I would do. I'd ask this girl to marry me before someone else beat me to it. Hell! He has already wasted a lot of time."

Frank did not waste any more time. He asked Anna to marry him that very night. They announced their engagement the following week. Frank asked Father David if he would officiate at the wedding ceremony but at the last minute he declined. A priest from St. Maries came up to the house in Harrison for the wedding. "I never married someone in a house that was haunted."

"Was haunted?" Anna replied. "I assure you, Father, the ghost of Jolie still dwells in this house. I am sure that she is watching us right now."

"Have you seen her?" he asked looking around the room.

"No." Anna looked around the room. "But I am sure she is present in this house tonight. I am disappointed that Father David could not make it. I heard he was released from the hospital weeks ago."

"He had a family tragedy. His brother was killed by a hit-and-run driver just last week. The police are looking for an old pickup truck. It's probably a drunk driver again but this is worse - the pickup truck was stolen. Anyway Father David is trying to find a new bank president."

As they walked away Frank felt Anna grip his hand tightly. "I bet it was Willy who drove that truck."

Frank leaned down and whispered, "Let's not try to solve that mystery. At least not tonight."

At the wedding reception as the guests were leaving, Anna spotted Carol Potter standing by Jolie's grave. Anna took her a vase of the wedding flowers from a table in the living room and went out to the grave. She knelt for a moment beside Jolie's grave and placed the flowers across it.

"She will like that," Carol said. "Someday I want to be buried here beside her."

"Carol, tell me what happened. I'm certain the Jolie must have killed Ethan. Did she do that after you and Amiee left?"

The old woman shook her head. "Ethan told us we had to leave the house. We expected that. David had warned us that his father was going to remarry and his uncles were moving back to Montana. What we didn't expect was to be turned penniless out into the street. Ethan knew every place where we hid money or valuables. He took it all. I remember Amiee put up a fight and he beat her severely. He was a small man, but he struck like a hammer and had a carpenter's grip that Amiee could not break free of. I ran and hid in my room. I was holding the door shut when Jolie appeared at the closet. I never did figure out how she did that. She told me not to put up a fight but to invite Ethan into my room and use what she called my golden charm to get him into my bed."

"Screw the little man until he is exhausted and I will do the rest," she told me and then she went back into the closet.

"Ethan was eager. I didn't have to give him much encouragement at all. He must have envied his brother for it felt like he was trying to make up a lost year. Finally he tired and Jolie came quickly out of the closet with her silver dagger. I put the bolster pillow over his head."

Carol shuddered. "He struggled so. His short arms and legs thrashing independently like they belonged to four different men. Jolie must have stabbed him a dozen times before he lay still."

Carol looked back at the house Frank and Connie were waiting silently on the porch.

"What else happened?" Anna asked.

"Only God knows how killing him affected us. When Jolie stepped down from the bed, her body was shaking like a wet dog. 'You had to do it,' I said. 'You did it for all of us.' We took back the money and jewelry he had taken from us. That is when I saw Jolie's blue-diamond necklace. I asked where she had gotten it, but she wouldn't tell me. We put the dwarf in my trunk and carried him out to the carriage house. The next morning we dug a grave for him. That was when the fire started."

Anna hugged Carol. "It's over."

"Yes, I wanted to tell Connie all this but I don't think I can. 'There is no statute of limitations on murder,' she told me in her official Judge Parker voice. 'You had better keep any tales of the house in Harrison to yourself.'"

"Why did Jolie stay?" Anna asked.

"It was just like when we left France. Jolie just took control. We did whatever she said."

Carol raised her head and looked out over the lake as she continued her story.

"The next morning by the first light of day, Jolie selected a spot near the carriage house where the ground had few rocks and we began to dig a grave. Jolie, Amiee and I each took a turn. I was waist deep in the grave when Jolie said she smelled something strange in the air. Smoke. Wood smoke. We walked to the crest of the hill. Hugh orange flames leapt from the building of the Grant Lumber Company, one of the biggest mills along the lakefront. At first the smoke rose straight up in the air like a tall dark cloud; then it mushroomed, rolling over and over upon itself. Even as we watched the fire spread to other buildings and stacks of lumber, Jolie quickly dragged the body of the dwarf into the shallow grave and began filling the dirt on top of him. By the time we had covered the body in the makeshift grave, a breeze rose off the lake and carried the smoke south over the town. It hugged the hillside all the way up to the unfinished grave. We rushed back to the mansion, packed a few things and started to run down the hill to the town. The smoke was too thick and we retreated to the house and hid there waiting to die."

Anna took Carol's hand, "You did escape. Did Amiee also?"

"Yes, we both escaped, thanks to Jolie. It was her plan. She talked the deacon's wife into helping us. She told her that the fire had put the fear of God in our hearts. We were going to leave our wanton ways behind. The woman gave us poor cloth to wear and we gave her some of our silk dresses. Jolie told her that we were afraid that the men who brought us here would try to follow and bring us back so we were going to dig three graves and she was to tell whoever asked that we perished in the fire. The woman was more than eager to help. She even arranged for the three coffins. We worked all night digging those graves. Amiee and I went down to purchase tickets for Coeur d'Alene on the steamer Ferrell. Jolie waited for the grave markers to arrive. She wanted to be sure they were placed right. Why I didn't understand."

"She hid her blue-diamond necklace in one of the graves and she planned to come back for it," Anna replied.

"It cost her. The first two men off the Ferrell when it arrived were Samuel and David Marshall. They walked right past us in our poor clothes. Jolie must have still been at the house when they arrived."

"So she hid from them," Anna said to the grave. "It must have been terrible all those years in the darkness."

Chapter 24

Frank and Anna left for Montana that fall. Every week Anna wrote her family to assure them that she and Frank were doing fine. They planned to return home for Christmas but the first week in December Frank received a letter from his grandmother, Carol, saying the Father David had died and he would be buried in a grave next to Jolie's at the house in Harrison. Because of class commitments Frank and Anna could not make it to Spokane in time for the funeral mass but they did arrive in Harrison before the procession arrived.

The road was wet with snow and Frank drove only as far as the carriage house. "With this fresh snow I could drive off the road bed and get stuck," he told Anna.

She jumped from the car. "Oh Frank! Doesn't it look grand?"

Frank nodded. Only a foot path in the snow led to the porch and the grand house. Every light in the house was shining brightly giving the house a look of splendor against the grey winter sky.

Anna hurried up the path when she saw Elizabeth standing on the porch. Frank walked over to the grave that had been dug beside the carriage house. "Jolie, you will soon have a neighbor. You see, he did come back for you."

Ten minutes later, the lead car in the funeral procession made its way up the narrow road. Frank opened the door to the carriage house and let the driver park inside. The Hearst parked directly in front of the carriage house. After that the cars just pulled to the side of the road and stopped. Frank walked out toward the road and started to direct the drivers of the other cars to park as they could on the road and not try to come up any closer. He found his grandmother and helped her walk up the muddy road to the carriage house.

"He must be a popular man in Spokane," Frank observed. "I can't believe that many cars came all this way."

"We will have to wait for them," Carol replied.

It was almost twenty minutes later with the casket was carried to the grave side and the services began. Frank, Carol and Anna walked over to the grave side and stood across the grave from Father David's family.

It began to snow lightly and Frank went over to his car and got Anna's winter coat. He helped her put it on and then looked up at the house. "You have lost a bit of your splendor."

"What do you mean?" Anna asked.

Frank gave her a hug. "I meant the house. One of the lights on the second floor just went out."

"Oh that's Amiee's room. The light never stayed on in the room anyway."

Frank stepped back. *Amiee's room? Yeah, I remember the lights flickered when I put them in that room. I was going to check that. Guess it blew a bulb.*

Four different priests took part in the ceremony. When the last "AMEN" was said Frank looked up again at the house. *Now two of the lights are off. What's happening?*

Frank slipped past his grandmother and stepped around the open grave. A third window in the house went dark. He raised his hand and pointed at the house. Others turned to look. Smoke billowed from two of the windows on the second floor.

"Fire!" The cry went up from several people at once. A feeling of despair ripped through Frank. "No. Not now."

There was nothing to do but watch as flames engulfed the old house. Bright orange lights filled the first two windows that had gone dark. Anna held tightly to Frank and cried. The fire spread to the top floor and the main floor with lightning speed. Everyone was rushing to their cars only to find the way down the hill blocked by the cars below them.

By night fall, a black shell was all that remained of the house in Harrison. Frank and Anna stayed with her parents that night and planned to drive back to Montana in the morning. Before leaving they walked hand in hand up to the house in Harrison for one last good-bye.

Volunteer firemen stood watch all night on the smoldering structure. Anna walked with Frank as close to the house as they felt was safe.

"Where will Jolie go now?" Frank asked.

"Wherever David Marshall leads her."

"Now Anna."

"But Frank, you were right. She was waiting for him to come for her and he finally did."

Anna reached her hand up behind Frank's neck. He leaned down and kissed her. "So now you are the romantic."

"Last night I had a dream. At least I thought it was a dream. Jolie came into my room and told me that she was leaving with David and then she gave me her blue-diamond necklace."

Frank laughed.

Anna reached into her coat pocket and took out the necklace. It glistened brightly in the grey winter light. "Jolie said that I was to give it to you. Yours was the first voice she heard after fifty years of silence."

Frank took it in his hands. He felt every stone, every link of the chain. "This is unbelievable. It is just as I imagined it."

He held it up to Anna. "Put it on. It's yours."

"Am I to be your mistress?"

"Of course, you're my wife."

Anna fastened the necklace around her neck. "A wife and mistress too. I can handle that."

Printed in the United States
69014LVS00001B/1-99